THE FROLIC
of the
BEASTS

Yukio Mishima was born in Tokyo in 1925. He graduated
from Tokyo Imperial University's School of Jurisprudence
in 1947. His first published book, *The Forest in Full Bloom,*
appeared in 1944, and he established himself as a major
author with *Confessions of a Mask* (1949). From then until
his death, he continued to publish novels, short stories, and
plays each year. His crowning achievement, The Sea of Fertility tetralogy—which contains the novels *Spring Snow* (1969),
Runaway Horses (1969), *The Temple of Dawn* (1970), and *The
Decay of the Angel* (1971)—is considered one of the defini-
tive works of twentieth-century Japanese fiction. In 1970,
at the age of forty-five and the day after completing the last
novel in the Fertility series, Mishima committed *seppuku* (rit-
ual suicide)—a spectacular death that attracted worldwide
attention.

INTERNATIONAL

ALSO BY YUKIO MISHIMA

THE SEA OF FERTILITY,
A CYCLE OF FOUR NOVELS

Spring Snow

Runaway Horses

The Temple of Dawn

The Decay of the Angel

Confessions of a Mask

Thirst for Love

Forbidden Colors

The Sailor Who Fell from Grace with the Sea

After the Banquet

The Temple of the Golden Pavilion

Five Modern Nō Plays

The Sound of Waves

Death in Midsummer

Acts of Worship

THE FROLIC
of the
BEASTS

THE FROLIC
of the
BEASTS

Yukio Mishima

TRANSLATED FROM THE JAPANESE BY
Andrew Clare

VINTAGE INTERNATIONAL
Vintage Books
A Division of Penguin Random House LLC
New York

A VINTAGE INTERNATIONAL ORIGINAL, NOVEMBER 2018

English translation copyright © 2018 by Andrew Clare

All rights reserved. Published in the United States by Vintage Books,
a division of Penguin Random House LLC, New York, and distributed in
Canada by Random House of Canada, a division of Penguin Random House
Canada Limited, Toronto. Originally published in Japan
as *Kemono no Tawamure* by Shinchosha, Tokyo, in 1961.
Copyright © 1961 by Yukio Mishima Estate.

The Cataloging-in-Publication Data is on file at the Library of Congress.

Vintage International Trade Paperback ISBN: 978-0-525-43415-3
eBook ISBN: 978-0-525-43416-0

Book design by Christopher M. Zucker

www.vintagebooks.com

Printed in the United States of America

THE FROLIC
of the
BEASTS

Prologue

It's hard to believe this photo was taken a few days before the final wretched incident. The three of them looked really happy, at ease with one another, as if there was a bond of mutual trust among them. The photo had been sent right away to the chief priest of Taisenji temple, who cherishes it even now.

Ippei Kusakado, dressed in a white *yukata* with black abstract patterns, Yūko, in a white dress, and Kōji, wearing white trousers and a white polo shirt, stood on the harbor wall by the shipyard warehouse under the strong summer sunlight, which was reflected back on them off the sea below. Only their suntanned faces stood out in relief against the even whiteness of the scene; and while the picture was sharp, a faint agitation filled the frame, making it seem a little out of focus. That wasn't surprising, since they had given the camera to the boatman and had him photograph them from the small boat; a certain amount of camera shake was unavoidable, no matter how calm the water.

They were in a small fishing port in West Izu called Iro, which was on the east side of a deep inlet. To the west, abutting the mountains, the inlet stretched out a number of feelers, each of which was cradled by the valley. There was a shipyard, albeit small in scale, oil storage tanks, and two or three warehouses storing netting and other equipment used by the fishermen.

The inland road didn't reach that far, so the locals had to come and go by boat from the shipyard to the oil storage tanks, and again from the oil storage tanks to the warehouses.

The three had put out from the harbor in a small boat, and the harbor wall they climbed for the photograph belonged to the warehouse.

"Over there looks perfect. Let's take it over there!"

Yūko, who was standing in the boat resting a parasol against her shoulder, had already indicated the spot and called out instructions from a distance. The August fishing season holiday was almost at an end; many fishermen had already begun setting off toward Hokkaido and the Sanriku coast to fish for Pacific saury, so there were far fewer boats in port than the previous week and the surface of the small inlet suddenly appeared larger than before.

It wasn't only the fishermen who had departed. Both Kiyoshi, who had been on leave from the Self-Defense Forces, and Kimi, who worked in the factory of Imperial Instruments, like Matsukichi—who had gone Pacific saury fishing—left their hometowns and returned to Hamamatsu. The short summer romances had come to an end and the new ukulele, inscribed with English lettering, was probably right at this moment resting on Kiyoshi's knees in his barracks room.

Kōji gave Ippei a helping hand up, and as the three ascended the harbor wall, this corner of concrete, which had been exposed to the harsh lingering heat of the day, appeared to lose in an instant—through the agency of this human intrusion—the delicate order, the poetic arrangement of its inert solidity, which it had so far preserved.

In front of the warehouse, nets had been hung carelessly on bamboo drying racks, forming a suitable picture frame for the surrounding scenery. A mast, now lying on its side; coiled lengths of stern rope. The whole scene implicitly related in its stillness memories of a voyage and of rest following hard work. The quiet breathing of the gentle breeze in the still sunlight, the great warehouse door painted sky blue, summer grasses growing thick and lofty between the warehouses, spiderwebs suspended between the grass stems, and the white flowers of wild chrysanthemum growing resplendent from among the cracks in the concrete. Pieces of red rail, rusty wire, the lid of a live-box, and a small ladder . . .

It was frighteningly still, and from where they stood gazing down, images of clouds and mountains were calmly reflected in the sea. The water close to the wall was especially pellucid and clearly revealed a shoal of small fish as they passed pale clumps of weeds. The white reflection of summer clouds broke into a thousand pieces close to the shore.

As she walked over the nets laid out to dry on the ground, Yūko stopped suddenly, having noticed what appeared to be droplets of blood scattered on the dazzlingly reflective surface of the concrete.

Realizing straightaway what it was, Kōji explained, "It's iron oxide. Probably spilled while they were painting something."

As the trembling shadow of Yūko's parasol moved over the splotches of paint, they turned a blackish red.

"Over there would be good," said the youthful Kōji, as he

took charge and positioned Ippei and Yūko in front of the first warehouse; Yūko complained that the fishing nets would conceal their lower halves.

"That's perfect," cut in Kōji shortly. "It's more artistic that way. Like we're three fish caught up in a net," he added, and began adjusting the camera he'd taken down from his shoulder.

It was exactly as Kōji had said, thought Yūko. The three of them—three fish caught in a net of sin . . .

As he was being positioned, Ippei, as always, did as he was told, as always, with a smile. Ippei was forty years old. He had a lean though regular face with a very rosy complexion. He walked with a limp on his right side, and his movements appeared somewhat sluggish, which at times actually made him look elegantly refined. He had the diligence of his wife to thank for his personal cleanliness, which was thorough, to say the least. It was also plain to see on closer inspection that he wore that interminable smile reluctantly, as though he were constantly perplexed with something. His *yukata* and sash, despite Yūko's careful attentions, always looked as if they were about to slip and drag down by his knees, not simply because he appeared unaccustomed to wearing the garment; rather, body and clothing gave the impression of moving away from each other entirely of their own accord.

Supporting her husband, Yūko turned to face the glaring direction of the camera. Struck directly by the sunlight, her face lost its relief and became like the vacant clear surface of a mirror. She was round-faced, and despite her generously proportioned good looks, her lips were thin. And while she seemed able to hide any amount of suffering with a slight application of makeup, panting in the heat, it also appeared that her mouth was emitting silent and invisible flames of anguish. In short, Yūko wasn't made to conceal her suffering. Her large, misty eyes, ample cheeks, soft earlobes, and even her smile, which displayed a certain ennui when she responded to Kōji, were all evidence of the anguish she experienced within. Yet Yūko did not appear tired, and this spoke volumes about her stubborn resistance to suffering.

"How much longer do we have to wait?" She folded her parasol, asking the question in her typically sensuous voice, which conjured up the image of a small, stifling room filled with fetid flowers.

Kōji reached out from the wall and, explaining the shutter action as he did so, passed the camera to Teijirō, the old boatman, who was standing on top of his vessel. Clad only in short pants, revealing his dark nakedness, Teijirō positioned his towel-wrapped head above the camera's viewfinder, like he was searching for a fish in a glass tank. Kōji's deportment in leaping over to the couple, who were now in front of the warehouse, was truly agile. The single unbroken line formed by his white trousers and white polo shirt flexed and snapped as if it were steel wire. He sidled over to where Yūko was standing and, in a completely natural manner, slid his arm around her smooth shoulder. At which point Yūko, out of natural consideration, took her husband's right arm from the left side, where he was standing, and placed it around her own shoulder.

"It's bright, isn't it?" said Kōji.

"Just a little longer."

"Yes, just a little longer."

Yūko cooed like a pigeon and suppressed her laughter, working hard not to ruin her expression for the camera as she said through partially open thin lips, "How marvelous it would be to erect a tomb like this—the three of us lined up together . . ."

Maybe the two men didn't catch what she said, for they didn't reply. Below them on the boat, Teijirō was still carefully getting the camera ready. He fought to resist the boat's swaying, bracing his legs firmly against the deck, the exertion of which caused the muscles on the old fisherman's shoulders to bulge and shine in the brilliant sunlight. Despite the quiet, the noise of the water was minutely woven in with the air, and the sound of the shutter didn't reach the ears of those being photographed.

While Iro is the archetypal fishing village, several fields and rice paddies extend close to the mountains in the east. If one travels awhile past the post office, the row of houses peters out and the road goes straight in the direction of the village shrine, running through the rice fields. Turning right along the way, a single road joins the slope and gradually rises up to the new graveyard, which lies on the mountainside.

A stream flows at the base of the mountain by the graveyard, and from alongside the stream, the graves begin, lying on top of one another, mazelike, reaching halfway up the slope. The farther down the mountainside one goes, the bigger and more magnificent the tombstones. From there the road becomes a narrow path made of pebbles and meanders up the hill, zigzagging its way in front of each row of tombs. The stone wall in front of the tombs has begun to crumble, and stout summer grasses have rooted themselves firmly between the gaps in the collapsed stone. A dragonfly spreads its dry wings and lies still, like a preserved specimen, on the hot stone. A medicine-like smell is in the air, the water in the vases having turned rank. In this region, the inhabitants use not bamboo or stone for vases but sake and beer bottles half buried in the ground, many of which are now filled with the withered branches of the Shikimi tree. If one climbs to this spot before the summer sunset—provided one can tolerate the vast number of striped mosquitoes—the view of Iro Village is superb. Taisenji temple can be clearly seen below, beyond the green rice fields. Farther in the distance, toward the south-facing mountainside, the broken glass windows of the abandoned Kusakado greenhouses twinkle as they catch the light. By the side of the greenhouses, the tiled roof of the now uninhabited Kusakado family house is visible. To the west, a black cargo ship glides past the lighthouse and slips into the port of Iro bay. Maybe it's a small cargo vessel from Osaka, laden with ore from the mines of Toi, on its way to anchor for a while in Iro harbor. The ship's mast comes silently past the rooftops, and the surface of the evening sea, faintly brighter than the beacon from the lighthouse, appears only as a narrow band from here.

A television can be heard clearly from a house somewhere in the village. The hail of a loudspeaker, belonging to the fishing cooperative, echoes around the surrounding mountainside: *"To all crew members of the* Kokura Maru. *Assemble here tomorrow after breakfast. We are preparing to sail!"*

One can discern the onset of night by the beam of the lighthouse, increasing in brightness hour after hour. The light is failing fast, so that the inscriptions on the gravestones become barely visible. It's difficult to locate the Kusakado grave, hidden in a corner among many other intricate tombstones. In spite of opposition from the majority of the villagers, the chief priest of Taisenji temple had erected the graves as requested, using the money entrusted to him. Three small new gravestones stand huddled together in a shallow depression in the hillside. To the right is Ippei's grave. To the left of that, Kōji's, and in the center lies Yūko's. That Yūko's grave appears charming and somewhat brilliant even in the twilight is because only hers is a living monument—a reserved burial plot—with her posthumous Buddhist name painted in bright vermilion. The vermilion is still fresh, and when it grows dark around the cluster of white gravestones, only the inscription is visible, appearing like the thick lipstick she always wore on those thin lips.

Chapter 1

Kōji thought about the sunlight that shone brightly into the connecting corridor that led to the bathhouse, cascading over the windowsill, spreading out like a sheet of white glossy paper. He didn't know why, but he had humbly, passionately loved the light streaming down through that window. It was divine favor, truly pure—dismembered, like the white body of a slain infant. Leaning against the handrail on the upper deck, he marveled at how the abundant early-summer morning sun that his body now comfortably soaked up was at this very instant, in some remote place, joining with the small, exalted, and fragmented sunlight of his memories. It was difficult to believe that this sunlight and the other were of the same substance.

If he were to trace the diffuse light in front of him, as though reaching hand over hand for a great, sparkling banner, would he eventually touch the tip of a hard, pure tassel of sunlight?

And if so, was that pure tassel tip the far, far end of the sunlight? Or was it the distant origin itself of the abundant sunlight right in front of him?

Kōji was traveling aboard the *Ryūgū Maru* 20, which had departed from Numazu bound for West Izu. The back-to-back benches on the upper deck were sparsely occupied, and the canvas awning sang in the breeze. On the shore, fantastically shaped rocks soared precipitously like a black castle, and high above in the sky, bright cumulus clouds drifted about in disarray. Kōji's hair was not yet long enough to be disturbed by the persistent wind.

He had regular and firm features, and his somewhat old-fashioned warrior's face and relatively bony nose made him appear like someone whose emotions were easily controlled. But his face was capable of hiding things. *My face is like a well-crafted, carved wooden mask*, he thought when he was in good humor.

There wasn't much pleasure in smoking a cigarette while bearing the brunt of the wind, for it soon deprives the mouth of both the taste and the fragrance of the smoke. But Kōji didn't remove the cigarette, continuing to draw deeply on the butt until a strange and bitter sensation filled the back of his head. He had no idea how many he'd smoked since leaving Numazu at nine thirty that morning. He couldn't stand the dazzling pitch and roll of the sea. To his unaccustomed eyes, the vast view of the world around him was nothing more than a vague, widely shining, and remote series of linked objects. He turned his thoughts back once more to the sunlight.

There was nothing more tragic than seeing the miraculous sunlight divided into four by the black window frame. Although Kōji loved the sunlight, having joined the crowd by its side, he had always just quickly passed it by. Ahead was the bathhouse, in front of the entrance to which he and his fellow prisoners had first formed a queue and waited their turn. From inside, a cheerless buzzer sounded at three-minute intervals, accompanied by the vigorous sound of water. Despite the powerful reverberation, the sound of the turbid, heavy water vividly brought to mind a rank liquid the color of dead leaves.

The numbers one to twelve were written on the floor in green paint, in double horizontal columns close to the entrance to the spacious changing room. Twenty-four men lined up by these numbers to wait their turn. Three-minute-interval buzzer . . . The slosh of water. A moment of quiet, then the sound of smacking flesh as somebody slips and tumbles on the wet floor, followed by a burst of laughter, which quickly subsides. Three-minute-interval buzzer . . . The men who had been waiting undress together and, having deposited their clothes on a shelf, move forward and line up over the two rows of horizontal numbers in front of the bathhouse entrance. Those numbers were painted yellow.

Kōji noticed the soles of his bare feet were neatly within the circle of the painted number. The inmates who had been standing in exactly the same spot three minutes earlier were now immersed in the bathtub. Steam, billowing out from the bathhouse, faintly enveloped Kōji's naked body: the muscles of his lower thorax, sparsely covered with hair, his flat stomach, and, below this, his hanging shame surrounded by a dark tangle of hair. It was a limp, drooping shame and resembled the carcass of a dead rat caught up among flotsam in a stagnant stream. He considered this: *I have converged shame from around the world and acquired this slightly dirty bundle, in much the same way as if I might have acquired a single point of light having converged with a lens the sun's rays.*

He gazed at the ugly backside of the man standing in front

of him. The world before his eyes was entirely obscured by ugly, pimple-covered backs and backsides. The door did not open. The soiled flesh door did not open. Three-minute-interval buzzer . . . The sound of water. Many backs and backsides began to stir, moving as one through the steam, before plunging into the midst of the great, narrow bathtub. Immersed up to their necks in the tepid, foul-smelling, murky water, everybody fastened their gaze on the hourglass on the warden's table. The three-minute flow of fine cinnabar granules appeared and disappeared amid the billowing steam. Bathing, washing, renewed bathing, exit. A red lamp glowed dimly close to the letters "Bathing."

Kōji remembered the hourglass clearly, and he recalled the stench of the water as it had clung tenaciously to his body— and the delicate cascade of cinnabar that flowed beyond the steam. He had been fascinated by the strangely quiet way the granules wholeheartedly flowed through the slender glass neck and unceasingly undermined themselves from within. The close-cropped heads of twenty-four people floating in the middle of the dirty water. Their grave expressions. Immersed in the water with serious, animal-like eyes. That's exactly how it was. Among all the trivialities of the prison, there existed something with a marvelously pure sanctity. That hourglass was also sacred. The cinnabar granules ran out. The warden pressed the button, and again the cheerless buzzer sounded. The prisoners stood up all at once, and many wet, hairy thighs advanced toward the duckboards. There was no sanctity at all in the sound of the buzzer . . .

The boat sounded its whistle twice. Kōji walked in the direction of the wheelhouse and gazed through the glass door at a young steersman wearing short rubber boots and jeans. The steersman sounded the whistle again, pulling with one hand on the white knob of a cord hanging from the ceiling while turning the brightly polished brass steering wheel with the other. The boat made a detour and began its entry into the port of Ukusu. To one side lay a narrow, sprawling, gray town. A Shinto shrine gate appeared as a single spot of red on the round mountaintop. In the harbor, an ore factory's cargo crane extended its arm toward the glaring sea.

Kōji was telling himself, *I have repented. I am a different person now.* This thought had likely as not been repeated countless times, always with the same rhythm, and as always it took the form of a resounding incantation. *I have repented* . . . In this way, even the freshness of the West Izu coastline became entwined in Kōji's penance—the crispness of the scenery itself, the verdure of the mountains, and the very clouds that, in Kōji's eyes, appeared to be quite detached from reality. For it was easy to believe that it ought to be so in the eyes of one who had repented. This notion had, like a single bacterium, nested itself in Kōji's body one day while he brooded in his cell, surrounded by bars, within the prison walls. And then, in an instant it had reproduced, until his flesh became riddled with remorse, his sweat, too, became the sweat of repentance, even his urine. Even the odor emitted by his youthful body became for Kōji the odor of repentance. It was a cold, gloomy, though in some ways also clear and bright—and yet extremely physical—odor. The odor of stable litter for an animal—repentance.

The ground above the shore gradually took on a yellow tinge with green pine trees dotted here and there, and this changing scenery signaled that the boat, which had left Ukusu, was now approaching Koganezaki. Kōji descended a flight of steps and went to the stern. A crowd of children had gathered around one of the ship's crew, who was making a half-hearted attempt to catch fish. He threaded an artificial fly onto a length of fishing gut, to which he then secured some hemp line before casting the lot far out into the sea. In a flash, the fishing gut leapt out through the air, glittering as it went, and then sank beneath the surface of the water.

Before long a saury was caught. The fish, which resembled a large horse mackerel, was reeled in, its hard belly thrashing against the unyielding water with a metallic ring. The fish having been landed, Kōji no longer felt the urge to watch it as it lay in the man's hand, and he transferred his attention to the sea.

Over to the left, the bare reddish-brown cliffs of Koganezaki loomed into sight from around the ship's prow. The sunlight cascaded down from the heavens directly above the cliff top and appeared like a smooth sheet of gold plate as it covered and illuminated every intricate undulation. The sea at the foot of the cliff was especially blue. The bizarre forms of the sharp rocks jostled with one another as they towered up out of the sea, and the swelling, upward-surging water turned into fine white threads before flowing down again from every crag and corner.

Kōji watched a seagull. It was a magnificent bird. *I have repented, I . . .* and he began his reverie once again. The *Ryūgū Maru* 20 left Koganezaki behind and, turning in the direction of the next port, Iro, set out intently along the coastal sea lane. The lighthouse at the entrance to Iro harbor gradually came into view on the port side. Fronting the long, narrow bay, the rows of houses and the forested mountains seemed to overlap each other, merging into a single, flat picture. As the boat came farther into the bay, however, the sense of distance between objects and buildings quickly increased; between the ice-crushing tower and the ice plant, between the lookout tower and the house rooftops, and the congealed picture increasingly gained perspective as if it had been thinned with hot water. Even the dazzling surface of the inlet seemed to unfold, and the pale reflection of the concrete quay was no longer simply a line of white refined wax.

Standing slightly apart from those who had come to welcome the boat, a single figure waited under the eaves of the warehouse, a sky-blue parasol concealing her face. Kōji found it difficult to reconcile the vivid, charming image in front of him with the starved vision he had been desperately clinging to for so long. There was no reason to believe he had been starved of sky blue. But if he had been, it would have been the color of repentance.

Kōji understood perfectly well the significance of the color of the parasol to Yūko's welcome. She had carried the same one on that summer's day two years ago. The day of the quarrel in the front garden of the hospital. The unfeeling rendezvous, followed by an evening meal where barely anything was said. Kōji's subsequent sudden victory and Yūko's submission. And then the incident that occurred at nine o'clock that evening. But no matter how much he reflected on that day's events, there had been no indication when Yūko, under her sky-blue parasol, had taken a stroll together with Kōji at noon that the day would end in a night of bloodshed.

The color of that sky-blue parasol on the quay was not the color of starvation; it was without a doubt the color of repentance. As for that other kind of starvation—the deprivation of the flesh—that had been sufficiently satisfied the previous night in Numazu, thanks to the money Yūko had entrusted to the prison governor. Kōji was certain that Yūko had also tacitly wished that the money should be used in this manner. Late last night, he had sent for yet another girl. Sensing what he wanted, they were afraid. He woke up in the morning, sandwiched between the two, having been caressed carefully all over, out of a certain sense of fear. In the relentless morning light that came in through the inn curtain, he reached out his hand to touch the object that had continued to exist for so long as a vivid fixation in his mind's eye. The girls didn't notice and slept on uncomplaining. It was poor flesh that had been concealed within, the flower of a crepe myrtle, steeped in alcohol, the erosion of the soul for the moment in flesh form, a thing distant and unrelated to the recollections and notions of the prisoners.

As Kōji clambered up from the barge, Yūko saw before her a young man, more dauntless than she remembered, and while he was slightly leaner than before, he had lost none of his erstwhile vigor. Wearing a summer suit with an open-collared shirt, he waved a hand cheerfully while clutching a small briefcase in the other.

"You haven't changed," Yūko said, greeting Kōji and moving her parasol obliquely to one side. In the shadow it cast, Kōji noticed the dark grape luster of her characteristic thick lipstick.

"I'd like to talk a little before going on to the house," said Kōji in a slightly hoarse voice.

"Yes, I thought it would be nice to talk, but there are no cafes in the village," Yūko replied, and scanned the vicinity while describing a lazy arc in the air with the basket she held in one hand. Only two or three of the ship's passengers disembarked and they moved quickly away from the quay, surrounded by those who had come to meet them. The *Ryūgū Maru 20* lost no time in turning its prow and heading off toward the bay entrance, water rippling gently in its wake.

"It's the opposite direction, but shall we walk toward the bay? There's a patch of grass and some shady trees where we could talk."

As they began to walk, Yūko was seized with anxiety that it had been a mistake to take charge of this forlorn young orphan. Since deciding to care for him, she had not once experienced such a sense of trepidation, which was clearly therefore some sort of presentiment. She had even been censured for her rashness by the prison governor, who said he had never before heard of a case where a member of the victim's family had become the criminal's guarantor.

The governor appeared at first to believe that it was the result of Yūko's philanthropic sentimentality, and she eventually conceded as much.

"I believe it is what I ought to do. After all, what he did he did for my sake."

The governor had looked hard at her as she stood before him in her flamboyant attire. *What incorrigible arrogance. This tendency for a woman to want to draw into herself all the complicated origins of the crime is by no means a rare occurrence. She wishes to become the dramatic, aesthetic personification of the origin of the crime itself.*

This self-conceit that was on the point of drawing the world to its depths ought, so to speak, to be described as the conception of the spirit; there would be no room for man to interfere in such matters. The governor's dubious gaze clearly betrayed his thoughts: *This woman wishes to conceive everything. She has*

tried to store it all away in her disagreeably warm belly—everything;
even the crime and that prolonged period of remorse; the tragedy, and
the cities where men gather together, and even the origin of all man-
kind's behavior. Everything . . .

They walked in silence along the bank and gazed at the sea.
A thin film of purplish oil lay on the calm surface, and a sundry collection of rubbish—pieces of variously shaped timber, a
pair of *geta*, lightbulbs, food cans, a chipped rice bowl, a corn
cob, a single rubber boot, an empty bottle that had once contained cheap whiskey, and, in the middle, the skin of a small
watermelon that reflected the flickering color of daybreak in
its pale flesh—floated in the water at the very back of the
inlet.

Yūko pointed to a small grassy depression in the hillside
close to the dolphin memorial tower. "It's lunchtime already.
Let's have some sandwiches over there while we talk."

Kōji looked up with suspicion in his eyes. A name was on
the tip of his tongue, but he found it difficult to speak. Yūko
looked at his hesitant mouth as though it belonged to a totally
different person. He had become meek. He had forsaken himself, to an almost excessive degree.

"Ah, do you mean him?" She realized the nature of Kōji's
attempted question and answered genially. "He's at home
today, eating alone. We thought it better that way. Instead of
meeting you all of a sudden. Of course, he's so looking forward
to seeing you. He has mellowed as well, you know . . . like the
Buddha himself."

Kōji nodded uneasily. They reached the spot Yūko had
indicated, and while the view of the bay was beautiful, and
the sunlight filtering down through the trees pleasing to the

senses, it wasn't as tranquil as it had appeared from a distance. Below them in a corner of the bay several large sculling boats were being hauled up onto the shore. The huts of the ships' carpenters were clustered in the same area, and the noise of busy hammers working on newly constructed vessels, and the beelike drone of machine saws, rose up and echoed around the hillside.

Yūko produced a wrapping cloth from her basket, spread it out on top of a bushy convolvulus plant, and with lithe fingers took out a tea flask and some sandwiches. Her movements were natural and serene, but her fingers had, over the passage of time, become somewhat brown and finely cracked from the sun. As Kōji watched the dreamlike ceremony of Yūko's gentle, unhesitant movements, it struck him that he had still not grasped entirely the essence of her gentle nature. For Yūko did not display in the slightest the sort of bland, innocuous gentleness born of the fear of offending one with a criminal record, nor was she overawed by the crime itself, as society normally demands. And while it appeared that she was in a vulnerable position, she did not welcome him with a womanly sentiment. Neither was it the same as the intimacy that accompanies complicity in crime, or the overfamiliarity of the kind displayed by a mistress. In Yūko's case, it was something quite different, for despite the incident, her attitude toward him had not changed in the slightest. In that moment Kōji, too, realized that he ought not to have come here. But it was too late for such regrets.

Kōji and Yūko were both able to recognize their own reticence as clearly as if watching the quick movements of a shoal of fish inside a tank of water. Yūko wished to show some sympathy toward the anguish Kōji experienced in prison, but she was at a loss to know what to say without sounding insincere.

In the same way, Kōji felt bound to apologize for the violent changes he had wrought upon Yūko's life, while at the same time wanting to know where he stood. But then, what could he say that was appropriate?

He felt as though he were suffering from some intangible, incurable disease, the condition of which—life in that detestable prison—still lived on vividly in his mind. He continually felt on intimate terms with it. This condition was invisible to Yūko. Invisible, but its unpleasant odor was by no means imperceptible. Before long, Kōji felt obliged to begin talking, as cheerfully as possible, about his experiences in prison, in the same way a patient is fond of explaining an illness.

"There are no mirrors in prison," he began. "Of course, there's no need for things like that. But as it nears the time for you to get out you suddenly become worried about your face. How will it look to people on the outside? In short, a convict who's coming up for release doesn't simply want his discharge number, he wants his face back. But like I said, there are no mirrors. What you do is you stand a dustpan against the outside of the windowpane so that your face is reflected in the glass. And so, whenever you see a cell with a dustpan against the window, you know that the guy inside is due for release soon."

Yūko couldn't stand listening to the story, and midway through in a feigned attempt to fix her face she opened the compact she had taken out from her sash. She had glanced at her own face and then thrust the mirror in front of Kōji. "Take a look! You haven't changed one little bit. There are no shadows anywhere."

For Kōji, Yūko's choice of words was more of a neurotic response than pushing the mirror under his nose. "You haven't changed one little bit." They were frightening words.

The surface of the mirror was dusted over with powder. He pursed his lips and blew. Before he had time to see the tip of his unexpectedly magnified nose, his nostrils were stifled with the scent of the floating powder. He closed his eyes, intoxicated by the stinging sensation it produced.

The world he had been trying so hard to reach for so long opened up expansively before him. A world of powder. The reality that corresponded to his long-held fantasy sent forth a fragrance of the genuine article. The privilege of dreaming inside one's prison cell, which he thought had since passed, took on meaning again for the first time since his release. A world of powder, wrapped in silk, the dusky comings and goings of its scent always carrying with them that languid afternoon flavor. And if there were times when it drifted far away in the distance, there were also times when it suddenly appeared before one's very eyes. While that world flies away in a moment, it leaves its trace on the finger like the minute dusty scales of a butterfly's wing . . .

"Well? You haven't changed one little bit, have you?" Yūko's bare white arm snaked out through the patchy sunlight filtering through the trees and snatched the compact away from Kōji's hand.

The drone of the machine saws had stopped, apparently for the lunch break. The surrounding area had become extremely quiet, save for the insistent wing beat of a greenbottle flying low around the convolvulus flower. Likely as not it had hatched from a discarded rotten fish on the beach, and having eaten its fill and become fat, it was now flying about in something of a faithless manner. It was a splendid combination of silver and dirt, and of cold metallic brilliance and warm putrefaction.

Kōji imagined that before long he would probably become fond of entomology, although there was once a time as a young man when he never so much as looked at an insect.

"I'm sorry I wasn't able to visit even once. I often explained the reason why in my postcards, but it's the truth, believe me. I can't even leave the house for a night. It's his condition, you see. When you see him, I'm sure you will understand, too. He'd be in a real fix if I wasn't there all the time."

"You must be content," answered Kōji, offhandedly.

Yūko's reaction, however, was remarkable. Her richly proportioned face reddened, and from between her impatiently twitching thin lips came forth a torrent of confused words, like the discordant hammering of piano keys.

"Is that what you wanted to say? The first thing you wanted to say when you came out was that? Oh, it's awful. That's an awful way of putting it. If you say it like that, then it ruins everything. It gets to the point where I can't trust anything in this world. Promise you won't say it like that again—promise?"

Kōji inclined himself obliquely on the grass and regarded this beautiful woman's anger. It came from within and pushed her body around, and her large eyes no longer had the courage to look in his direction. He watched quietly. And as he did so, the serious implication of his words began to penetrate his extremities, like water gradually seeping into sandy ground. The truth was that they were not yet accustomed to one another. It was a dangerous situation, for although one would expect more of a false intimacy when man and beast conversed, the two of them were testing each other, sniffing one another—like two animals on their first encounter. They played as if fighting and fought as if playing. All the same, it was Kōji who was seized with fear, and despite her anger, Yūko remained undaunted. As if to prove as much, she smoothly changed the topic of conversation and began to tell him how she had closed down the Tokyo shop a year or so ago, moved to Iro Village, and started running the Kusakado greenhouse.

"Anyway, we need a man's helping hand around here. It means a lot of study and a lot of work for you. We've gained a pretty good reputation from our first batch of flowers produced this spring. Oh, and we've also started foliage plants from this May. The temperature regulation is a bit of a nuisance, but I think you will come to like this job. I think you . . . Yes, you've definitely got a peace-loving face now."

Having finished their lunch, they returned to the port, skirting around the bay. Once there they carried on through the center of the village, cut across the prefectural highway, and followed the road up to the Kusakado house. A number of villagers greeted Yūko, and passersby looked on with interest. Doubtless rumors would spread through the whole village by sundown. And naturally, while Yūko was prepared to cover for him and say that Koji was a relative, the villagers would be sure to discover the truth of the matter quicker than an ant tracking down sugar.

"Try not to walk with your head hanging down like that," said Yūko, cautioning him in an emphatically candid manner.

"I can't help it," answered Kōji, still with downcast eyes, and he watched the slightly distorted shadow of Yūko's parasol as it passed lightly over bus and truck tire marks impressed on the highway in the noon heat.

Moving directly east from the highway, if one turns left after passing the post office, the road gently winds its way in front of the gate of Taisenji temple and up the slope to the few scattered houses at the back of the hillside.

The Kusakado house was a single isolated building that showed off its unconstrained tiled roof from the highest point of the mountain. Its capacious gardens were buried in greenhouses.

At the top of the slope in front of the gate to the house stood a figure dressed in white clothes that were billowing in the wind. Yūko had recently erected a white painted wooden fence, twined with roses, where no gate had stood before, on the front of which she secured a large nameplate bearing the inscription "Kusakado Greenhouse." The white bundle of clothing belonging to the figure was undoubtedly a *yukata*, though due to the wind and also the slovenly way in which it had been thrown on, the hem flared out like a skirt, and the ramrod-straight figure appeared as unnatural as if it had been encased in a plaster cast.

Owing to the weight of the case he held at his side and the ascent of the gentle slope, Kōji's brows were moist with sweat. Yūko's fingertips lightly touched his side and held him back. Looking up for the first time, he was seized with fear—as though the prison chaplain himself was waiting there to receive him again.

It was Ippei; the first time Kōji had seen him since that day. The high-noon sun cast dark shadows over a corner of Ippei's face, making it appear as though he was welcoming his guest with a harsh, defiant grin.

Chapter 2

Yūko knew full well just how much of a fun-loving, hotheaded youth Kōji had been two years earlier. Ippei had a Western ceramics shop in Ginza and during the busy seasons such as the summer holidays and year-end he hired students from his alma mater to work on a temporary basis. Kōji had measured up to Ippei's requirements, and he was able to continue the side job out of season, as well as being welcome at Ippei's residence in Shibashirogane.

Ippei had graduated with a degree in German literature, and after working for a while as a lecturer at another private university he inherited his parents' Ginza shop, where he continued to write highbrow literary critiques, for which he had acquired something of a reputation. His works were extremely few in number, but he had an avid following among his readers and his older books, which had since gone out of print, commanded high prices. He produced translations and commentaries on the works of authors like Hofmannsthal and Stefan George, and he had also written a critical biography of Li He. His literary style was exquisitely refined and displayed none of the businesslike aspects inherent to his ceramics trading, but instead was brimming with the cool eccentricity and embellishment characterizing a lover of art.

As a consequence of halfheartedly dabbling in spiritual matters, this kind of person tends unwittingly to acquire the privilege of contempt for the generality of spiritual activities otherwise unknown to the average human and becomes a strangely vacant and sensual being.

Right from the start of his side job, Kōji was astonished at how busy Ippei was with his love affairs. Of course, Kōji remained detached from these matters, which had nothing whatsoever to do with him. On one occasion, as he was about to finish work and go home, Ippei had been extremely friendly, calling him back and suggesting they go for a drink together. As soon as they were settled in the bar, Ippei began to talk.

"You haven't got any ties at all. I'm really quite envious. No parents, no brothers and sisters, nor relatives. Not even a wife and child. I detest people with splendid families and splendid guarantors. And tell me, I'll wager you have only enough money to get by on, don't you?"

"I think I can make do somehow until I graduate on the money my old man left me. But that on its own isn't enough."

"That's okay, isn't it? You can use what you earn in my shop as spending money."

"I appreciate it."

After a moment's silence, Ippei sipped his drink and said, "I heard you were involved in a fight a couple of days ago."

Surprised, Kōji stammered slightly: "H-how did you know that?"

"A store assistant heard the story from one of your colleagues; he thought it amusing and came to tell me."

Kōji scratched his head like an embarrassed schoolboy. Ippei demanded a full explanation, and so Kōji related how that night, after the shop had shut, he and a fellow part-time employee had gone for a drink at a whiskey bar in Shinjuku. As they left a fight began, and having quickly settled the matter, they made off. Ippei was much more interested in Kōji's state of mind than in the incident itself.

"Is it because you were annoyed? Did you do it because you were angry about something?"

"I don't really know why. I just lost my temper all of a sudden." Having never been questioned like this before, Kōji was at a loss to explain.

"You're twenty-one years old, all alone, so lighthearted, and so quarrelsome. Do you sometimes think yourself extremely romantic?"

Kōji pursed his lips and remained silent, sensing that he was being either ridiculed or afforded praise he didn't deserve.

"It's a good thing to be able to fight and express your anger. The future of the world is all but in your hands. After that, 'old age is all that awaits you.' There is nothing other than that."

This obscure quote from ancient poetry sounded terribly affected to Kōji. Ippei posed another question: "I suppose you never feel like the world sometimes slips out of your grasp and escapes from between your fingers like sand, do you?"

"Yeah, I do. And when that happens I start to get angry."

"Yes, but don't you see? That's one of your merits. For so long I have given in to that escaping sand."

Kōji resented being lectured on his senior's adulation of life and philosophical sentiments.

"In other words, what you're trying to say is that I'm just like everyone else?"

He drew a cynical conclusion in an attempt to bring the conversation to an end, and having done so, he glanced sideways at the face of this near forty-year-old wealthy man as it loomed up at him out of the dim light of the bar. Ippei, who had two suits made each month, was dressed in a sober necktie and a pale Italian silk shirt. In every respect he brought to mind the elegant appearance of the man in the French novel *L'homme couvert de femmes*. He went to a high-class hair salon; though he could afford to pay anytime, he held an account with a first-rate tailor, and out of a sudden fancy, he had obtained a pair of English-made spats, which he had grown tired of wearing almost immediately.

Ippei had everything. At least from Kōji's point of view, what he didn't possess wasn't worth mentioning. And while he may have lost his youth, he made use of the youth of others without reserve, greedily sucking on Kōji, doglike, until the very marrow of the bones had gone. Despite Ippei's largesse, Kōji didn't feel inclined to be his characteristic cheerful self. Kōji's cheerfulness was his well-oiled, well-maintained skates, the means by which he was able to glide along on the surface of life. With friends of the same age, he could ingratiate himself without anxiety. He enjoyed joining in with the families of such friends where compassion would be shown for his orphan status, where he could eat to his heart's content, and, above all, where he could behave in a slightly egotistical but nevertheless ebullient manner.

Society heaps praise upon those individuals who refuse to be prejudiced against the unfair treatment life has dealt them.

Indeed, it is deeply touched by the natural attitude to life displayed by these unnatural individuals. For Kōji, even a fight represented a semi-artificial impulse designed to elicit such praise. It was the expression of an attempt to behave normally in society, although he didn't consider it necessary to confide such secrets to Ippei. Indeed, was it necessary to impart more than he had already to Ippei? Ippei, who had everything.

On that particular night, Ippei and Kōji drank at the counter. A girl drew near like a shadow but left again, having been ignored by Ippei. The bartender attempted to strike up a friendly conversation, but Ippei didn't reply and so he moved off to chat with another customer. Dozens of liquor bottles lined up against the wall, cigarette smoke lingered like clouds, the soot-covered ceiling, the fragrance of perfume as girls moved to and fro in the narrow bar . . . A girl staggered over, on the point of collapse, gripped the far edge of the counter with her hands, and then proceeded to order another scotch soda for her customer in a slovenly tone of voice. Kōji was surprised by the warmth of her arm as it came into contact with his hand. The girl laid her cheek against her exposed forearm and gazed up at him out of drunken eyes.

"Pretending to do gymnastics, huh?" said Kōji.

"Ha, calisthenics more like."

The girl's hands were finely strained as they gripped the opposite side of the counter, her silver nails hooked firmly into the thick decorative padding on its side. She repeatedly bumped her large, white, pallid breasts forcibly against the counter's side.

"I feel really good," she said.

Kōji scanned her quickly pulsating body, her wholeheartedly debauched appearance, and her apparent enthusiastic embrace of alcoholic intoxication. It was all terrifying. She was laughing with large, expressionless eyes. Then suddenly she straightened herself, banged into Kōji's arm with her shoulder, and, seemingly transformed, walked away with a steady gait. In the space vacated by the girl, there lingered a kind of depression in the air created by her warm, generous body. It was like a wheel rut—utterly inflexible and everlasting . . .

"Now take my wife," Ippei said, as he deliberately drew the stem of his cocktail glass through his fingers. "She's a real odd case. I've yet to meet a stranger girl."

"Everyone at work says how pretty your wife is. But I've never seen her in the store."

Confronted by such flattery, Ippei gave the youngster an affected and supercilious look of contempt.

"Flattery will get you nowhere, my boy, at your age. I'm telling you she is odd. She's frightfully tolerant, and to this day has not once exhibited any jealousy. A wife, that is to say, if she is a normal type of girl, is jealous every time her husband breathes. You'll find out, too, when you get one yourself. But mine isn't like that. I've tried to scare her often enough. But she doesn't frighten at all. You could fire a pistol right in front of her eyes and she would probably just delicately turn her face aside. You may have heard it from the others, I've tried to make her jealous, I've tried everything, really I have."

"Maybe your wife is good at hiding her emotions. Maybe she has a strong sense of self-esteem, and . . ."

"How perceptive of you. A splendid analysis," said Ippei, attempting to thrust his extended index finger at the bridge of Kōji's nose. "Likely as not you've hit the nail on the head. But she hides it so cleverly, so perfectly. So you see, you would be grossly mistaken in thinking that she doesn't love me, because she does. She loves me terribly. She loves me with more than a wife's usual moderation. It's always the same gloomy, overly serious, stubborn frontal attack, always in that precise order. It's her army of love. A solemn army. And she always makes sure that I clearly see it march past, and then feigns indifference. I don't hate my wife. It's rather an embarrassing confession: I don't hate any woman who will love me. Even supposing it's my wife, do you see? I get awfully tired sometimes. This is all I wanted to tell you."

Ippei struck a match and lit an English cigarette with the deliberate composure of one who has just finished confessing all to one whose worth he values very little. There was something condescendingly tolerant about the way he struck the match, and Kōji hated it.

It is true to say that Kōji, who had yet to meet Yūko, fell in love with her that same night. And in all probability that, too, was a part of Ippei's plan. Kōji was clearly jealous of Ippei's corrupt heart. Notwithstanding this, his first impression of Ippei, having spent an evening with him in leisurely conversation, can only be described as insubstantial. Ippei was nothing more than a worthless, boring, middle-aged well-to-do playboy of the sort that can be found in any large city, and he had merely devised a slightly eccentric pretext for his dissipated lifestyle.

Early one particular afternoon close to Christmas, however, Kōji was surprised to find that the impression he had formed of Ippei during the latter's confession in the bar that night was belied by what he now saw. For Ippei, dressed in a good-quality suit, received his valued clients with cups of coffee, conversing with them as he nimbly went back and forth between shop front and office.

"If it were a gift of slightly higher quality, I could show you a Meissen plate or perhaps a Sèvres vase. Admittedly it's a little on the expensive side, but I'm sure if it is your good self, sir, you could manage it if you abstained from your customary drink for one night." Or, alternatively, "Ah, yes, a sixty-piece coffee set for a year-end gift, wasn't it? May I recommend our own gift paper? I guarantee, wrapped in this the item will appear at least three times its price . . ."

Kōji thought, *How on earth can someone possessing several volumes of his own literary work bring himself to say such a thing?*

Moreover, Ippei knew how to manipulate the provincial millionaires, using his reprimanding, pedantic tone to force purchases that exceeded the customer's expectations.

Kōji hadn't the faintest idea of the complex sequence of events behind Ippei's sometimes childlike, sometimes adult character—the injured self-pride (notwithstanding the way he spoke to his customers), which he always gloomily clung to, and which he believed, by some strangely fixed notion, would only be salved by Yūko's jealousy; his wife's refusal to cooperate in this, and her rejections; and his numerous, hysterical love affairs. Nor did Kōji understand the strange passion that tore Ippei between the servility of the dealer and the superiority of the intellectual while working to further the irreparable ruptures occurring in every aspect of his personal life and in his state of mind.

Kōji thought only of Yūko. He wasn't to know until much later how much of a hopeless love affair theirs would prove to be, and absorbed in his fantasy he formed an exceedingly simple schematic picture in his mind. First of all, there was a miserable, despairing woman. Then there was a self-indulgent, heartless husband. And last, a hot-blooded, sympathetic young man. And with that the scenario was complete.

That summer's day, which had begun with the assignation at the hospital—Yūko carrying her sky-blue parasol—and which had culminated in the incident at nine o'clock in the evening, took place some six months after Kōji had first met Yūko. That is to say, it occurred after he had taken a shop delivery around to Ippei's residence in Shibashirogane, where he first made her acquaintance.

The more frequent their meetings, the more Kōji felt driven to despair, right from the start of the days they were scheduled to meet. It was as if a cold torrent was beginning to flow clamorously in his innermost heart, and he hated himself more than he had done on any other morning. The request for a date would always come from him, and he would importune her before approval was eventually obtained. Moreover, Yūko would take him along only on shopping excursions, trips out for lunch, or else to a dance if he was lucky, and then she would promptly leave whenever it suited her.

On the morning of their last tryst, Kōji lifted his head out from under his quilt and gazed over at his university notebooks piled up on his desk, their voluminous open pages curling up in the summer sunlight as it came in through the window. As he did so he recalled the bundle of papers that Yūko, after considerable hesitation, had disclosed to him at their last meeting. The papers were a private investigator's report she had commissioned, a compilation of the names of Ippei's female acquaintances that detailed the name and address of one girl in particular—Machiko—as well as the fact that Ippei visited her every Tuesday evening.

"You must never tell my husband about this, do you understand? In any case, I'm content just knowing about it. It's just that, well, he mustn't find out I've checked up on him like this.

That's all I have to live for at the moment. Promise you will keep it secret? I shall die if you betray me."

That was the first time Kōji had seen Yūko cry. It wasn't a stream; on the contrary, the tears spread out faintly from the corners of her eyes and in an instant had become a sparkling thin film covering the whole of the surface. Kōji felt that, if he were to touch those tears, which had clearly been shed out of pride, his finger would freeze.

He recalled experiencing a dream at the time. In it, Ippei was gripped by a wild ecstasy, having seen the bundle of papers, and burning with conviction he determined to renounce all the other women and rush back to his wife's side. Once there, however, he discovered not his wife but her corpse. This quick drama had flashed across Kōji's mind in one noisy instant. It was like listening to the siren of an ambulance as it dashed along a deserted street late at night. Kōji almost lent a hand in the accomplishment of that tragedy.

"I'm going to go and visit someone in T Hospital at three," said Yūko, adding that Kōji should wait for her in the front garden of the hospital at three thirty.

T Hospital was a large, modern building located not very far from Ippei's residence. It stood roughly halfway up a south-facing slope in the middle of a residential area forming a valley, and a gentle, wide sloping driveway looped its way around the hospital to the front entrance. This newly built five-story hospital had an airy appearance, incorporating the piloti style of architecture, with glass-faced walls, white-tiled pillars, and blue-tiled window frames. There was a lawn on the south-facing slope of the front garden, as well as hemp palms,

Himalayan cedars, and a variety of shrubbery. Two or three benches had been set out, although nothing in particular had been provided to block out the intense sunlight of the summer afternoon.

With one side of his face exposed to the westerly sun, Kōji stared fixedly in the direction of the main entrance and felt as though the light were eating into his face like a red crab, leaving its imprint on his cheek. It was three forty-five, and there was still no sign of Yūko. A pair of kites was flying above the hospital. Cheerless fluorescent lamps shone from within the large, bright windows. One window was closed in by a set of glossy venetian blinds. Another displayed the shining silver of medical instruments. And by the windowsill a kettle was visible, and a red plastic toy.

Sweat dripped down the collar of Kōji's suit as he waited. He suddenly felt that what Yūko had told him about visiting someone in the hospital was a lie. Perhaps she'd come here in connection with her own condition. What if by some chance that corruption that had taken such a firm hold of Ippei had also rooted itself inside Yūko and inflamed her soul like a summer sunset?

A sky-blue parasol unfurled near the entrance. Like someone emerging into a heavy downpour, no sooner had Yūko stepped out from behind the large glass doors than she had opened her sun shade. *She's trying to hide her face*, thought Kōji, gloomily.

It was approximately thirty yards between the entrance and the bench, the two locations being intersected by a wide vehicle turnaround. He lacked the courage to fix his eyes on her slowly approaching form and averted his gaze toward the ground. Something by his feet caught his attention. It was a black wrench. It had doubtless been forgotten and left by somebody while they were repairing their car on the driveway.

Much later while in prison, Kōji repeatedly reflected on the discovery he made at that moment. That wrench was not merely something that had been dropped there; rather it was the manifestation of a material phenomenon making its sudden entry into this world. To all appearances, the wrench, which lay on its side half-buried in the overgrown lawn exactly on the border with the concrete driveway, looked all the more natural in its present position—as though it ought to be there. However, this was merely a splendid deception, for it was undoubtedly some other indescribable substance that had provisionally assumed the form of a wrench. Some form of substance that originally ought not to have been here at all; a substance that, having been excluded from this world's order, at times suddenly manifests itself in order to upset the very foundations of that order—the purest of pure substances. It was that substance that must have taken the shape of the wrench.

We normally consider "will" to be something intangible. Take, for instance, a swallow that skims past the eaves, the strange shapes of bright clouds, the sharp ridgeline of a tiled roof, lipstick, a lost button, a single glove, a pencil, or the hard fastener of a flexible curtain. We don't normally refer to such objects by the term "will." However, if we assume that not our will, but the will of "something" exists, then it would come as no surprise to find *that* "something" manifesting itself as some form of material phenomenon. While consciously working to upset our even, everyday sense of order, it becomes stronger, more unifying, waiting for the moment when it can integrate us into its own inevitably full and jostling system, and while it normally scrutinizes us from some invisible form, at the most critical moment it takes on shape and manifests itself as a tangible material object. *Where do they come from?* Kōji often conjectured, while brooding in his cell, that such objects probably came from the stars.

That was but a moment. He gazed intently at the black luster of the wrench. The moment was imbued with a quite inexplicable enchantment; time stood still and almost burst with the fascination of the wrench. Time was like a basket piled up with fruit. Thanks to that dirty, black, key-shaped piece of iron, a cool, mellow, charming fascination overflowed from the basket in a mere instant. Without hesitation Kōji picked it up and put it in the inside pocket of his summer jacket. It burned like fire and penetrated his shirt, pleasantly warming the flesh of his chest. Before long, the sky-blue parasol came closely into view, its stretched silk canopy raised aloft, and Yūko smiled wryly with thickly painted lips.

"Sorry to have kept you. I should think you were hot, weren't you? I should have let you borrow this."

She held her parasol against the back of the bench and blocked out the westerly sun. At that moment, Kōji had no reason at all to believe that Yūko had witnessed his strange behavior just now.

Kōji vividly recollected what they had discussed at length under the hot sunlight. To begin with, Yūko related how the condition of the patient she had just visited had improved considerably more than she had expected. Kōji listened without believing a word of it. Then, totally out of the blue, she said that she thought she had aged, a notion that Kōji enthusiastically denied.

"But when I look at my husband's face I don't think there's

any doubt about it," said Yūko, as always, gradually broaching the topic of conversation Kōji most disliked. Whenever she began talking about Ippei, she appeared to Kōji like a woman who was rapidly sinking in a swamp right in front of him. Before he even had time to reach out his hand, she had slipped between the open lotus flowers, feet, thighs, stomach, and then chest, instantly drowned in the mire, until even her thickly adorned thin lips disappeared, still wearing that smile, and afterward, all that remained on the surface of the swamp was a faint ripple of water.

Yūko told the story, which, incidentally, Kōji had already heard from time to time, of how much fun Ippei had been in his twenties; how he had been the personification of youth itself. That was evident in the long, enraptured commentary "The Vilification of Youth" that appeared in his biography of Li He, and at the time he wrote it, Ippei undoubtedly looked upon his own adolescence in the same light as the celestial man in that brilliant poem of the same name:

> *Astride a glittering saddle of gold,*
> *Atop a splendid, stout dapple-gray horse,*
> *Dressed in fine scented silk clothes,*
> *With a beautiful maiden in his arms,*
> *He discards the bejeweled cup,*
> *And the lowly people looking on exclaim,*
> *"He must be a celestial man!"*

The respect in which Kōji differed from Ippei could be simply expressed in the verse: *"He went through life without so much as reading a word."*

There was no reason why Yūko should have recited this poem while sitting on the bench drenched in the summer sun.

She had previously lent the book to Kōji, and she had in particular drawn his attention to this piece, which he read in the austere surroundings of his lodgings; he realized that the disagreeable line quoted by Ippei during their first conversation in the bar that night was the closing verse of the poem. The young Ippei had certainly not wanted for anything. But now everything he possessed had begun to emit the stench of decay. There was no reason to believe that Yūko had not detected this foul odor, but likely as not she had come to love its fragrance. Ever since Ippei had convinced himself that only good fortune was destined to come his way, the manner in which he lived his dreadfully affected and artificial lifestyle had become markedly conspicuous.

Ah! It was an unbearable topic of conversation for Kōji! What could he do to shut her up? He suddenly stood up, swung his arms around as if he was doing gymnastic exercises (the wrench, which had already cooled, repeatedly knocked against his chest), and then walked around and sat down on the back-to-back bench. This nonchalant reaction to what Yūko saw as a stolid conversation cut her deeply.

There was a moment of hot silence around the bench. The chirring of a cicada sounded from the hairy trunk of a hemp palm. Kōji felt the tip of one of the parasol's spokes stick slightly in his hair, but he left it as it was. A little while later, Yūko stepped in front of him, and stared down at him, still holding the parasol. Her face appeared slightly pale due to the shadow it cast.

"Why are you angry? What do you want me to do? You're so self-centered, what right have you got——"

"What right? Don't talk nonsense. Why don't you sit down?"

"I don't want to. It's so hot here."

The protest sounded extremely childlike.

"Well, if that's the case, please move out of the way. I'm trying to look at the view."

"I'm going home."

Yūko, however, did not go home. Feeling hurt by the certain knowledge this young nobody had of the hollow home to which she ought to return, Yūko, far from following her intentions, sat down beside Kōji on the scorching bench.

"Can't you leave that subject alone?"

"I have, haven't I?"

"It's annoying when you talk about him all the time."

"It's an uncomfortable topic of conversation for me, too, you know. It's not just you."

"You mean you talk about him involuntarily?"

"It's my song. Is it forbidden to hum a tune? It's my song I tell you."

"And you expect me to join in the chorus? You must be joking. It's a timid, cowardly song with only a bone-like shell of self-respect remaining."

Kōji's boorish choice of words was unsubstantiated by the facts. It was unclear when he had begun to use such uncouth language and at what point Yūko had chosen to overlook it. And there was no doubt that she welcomed those too-familiar youthful words as if she were being pleasantly stung with a light and pliant whip. In any case, Kōji was caught in a dilemma between the choice of language—which was constrained by an excess of familiarity—and excessive behavior, which was compelled by his emotions. While he was looking closely at Yūko's hot cheeks, there appeared to be between them, as always, a distance similar to that between the skin of a patient and her doctor.

It was a meaningless squabble that went round and round

in circles. Yet, because it was an honest anger, their heartbeats quickened. And then the anger quietly lost direction and gave way to a sense of common purpose . . . Kōji later wondered why, despite this confrontation, the quiet serenity of the surrounding scenery had remained etched in his memory.

The grassy south-facing slope commanded a view of the immediate locality—the three sides of the town in the valley, surrounded by hills that were covered with rows of houses, and on the summit of the hills stood sparse clumps of trees reaching up and almost touching the sky.

Closely built houses—some old, some modern—basked in the westerly summer sun and produced an unattractive, stark stereoscopic effect. The yellowish buildings of a junior high school soared precipitously in the east, while to the west could be seen an automobile firm, above which an ad balloon—displaying the names of new models of cars—hung in the sky like a sagging stomach. It was quiet, without a single solitary human form; a weary scene engulfed in the vast summer light. There were graves, too. Close to the summit, a narrow cemetery containing no more than a dozen or so tombstones, closed in on the house rooftops from above, looking like a group of cornered, naked refugees about to face the firing squad—backs against the cliff wall, standing on tiptoe, trembling with fear, huddled together in a state of paralysis, unable to help themselves.

Then came the evening meal, where they hardly said a word to each other. And afterward, Kōji's sudden victory and Yūko's submission. From that evening until nightfall, everything seemed to slide down like the flow of a dirty waterfall. After dinner they had gone to a small basement drinking house.

Yūko suddenly began to speak her mind, to which Kōji added strong rebuttals, and for the first time they quarreled to their hearts' content, stinging each other to the quick. Kōji accused Yūko of being spineless.

"You're just a weak-willed coward. You're afraid of facing up to reality. Of course, you want to know the truth, but you refuse to look at it with your own two eyes."

"That's a lie. It's just that the truth, when I do eventually face up to it, is bound to be worse than it is on paper. I would rather see Ippei lose his presence of mind. Seeing his impassive face, well, it would simply be the end."

"Well, if it's the end it's the end, isn't it?"

"What would a child like you know about it?"

Kōji became confused, losing track of where he was trying to lead Yūko. Was it not possible that in his passion he was trying to transform her into the woman Ippei desired her to be?

Even assuming it was so, he hated the monstrously grotesque reality of Yūko's obstinate refusal to change. And if it were something he could break down, even if the result meant the success of Ippei's stratagem, he would have to accept it.

"If that's the case, do you hate my husband? Or is it that you really hate me?" said Yūko, at length, her tone challenging.

"Maybe both of you. But maybe I hate the boss the most."

"You're a strange one, aren't you? Here I am, a lady of means and with a lover to boot, receiving a monthly allowance from my husband. Why can't I stay as I am? Even if I carry on like this, you won't suffer at all, will you?"

"It's because you tell lies. That's why we can't go on like this. I can't allow such lies, even if they are nothing to do with me."

And in this way Kōji finally showed his bright, youthful colors. Twenty-one-year-old Kōji—wearing a red military uniform and blowing his trumpet. He was able to behold his own portrait without being the least bit ashamed. Being in a position to openly scrape off the dark, worldly confusion of others was a privilege of youth, and after all, who could stand in his way?

Yūko, despite having drunk a considerable amount, fixed her pellucid eyes on Kōji's face. She looked like somebody who suddenly had thrust before them an incomprehensible picture or a map that was impossible to trace. She extended an elegant finger into the dusky light and, like a blind woman, reached out to touch his cheek, only to stop halfway. To Yūko, Kōji's cheek appeared to suddenly harden like stone. Her head was bent forward and a green-tinged shadow fell across her cheek, and in a terribly cold, almost possessed tone of voice she said, "Today is Tuesday."

What Kōji vividly remembered, more than the thirty-minute passage of time between eight thirty and nine o'clock that evening, was the stillness of the scene—almost as if it were a painting formed of living people.

It took place in an ordinary apartment. Ippei was sitting up on the bed at the back of the room, dressed in a silvery gray silk gown. At his feet sat Machiko, wearing an identical gown, her hands thrust in the pockets. They were both naked underneath. A stand-type electric fan generously waved its drooping neck above their heads. Since the apartment had been hastily arranged, the color and design of the curtains and furniture did not match. Unfinished drinks stood on the bed table together with an ashtray. A three-sided mirror with its wings spread out appeared as if it was about to swallow up the room. With his pallid, tired face, Ippei looked sick.

A little while after they had knocked, Machiko appeared at

the door, having adjusted the collar of her gown. Yūko slipped sideways into the room, followed by Kōji. Machiko drew back and sat on the bed, and Ippei quickly pulled his gown around him and propped himself up.

There was no great outcry or quarrel, events so far had run as fluidly as water—and then stopped; the four of them observed one another as if looking through a transparent glass wall, a glass wall that had suddenly been erected before their eyes, and that was extremely difficult to negotiate.

There was a marvelously surreal aspect to this truly wretched, mundane portrayal of reality. It was almost hallucinatory in its crystal clarity. Kōji recalled how the thoroughly creased sheet, which had appeared from beneath the displaced feather quilt, looked very much like a collection of lines drawn by an abstractionist depicting a diagram of movements.

There was something in the way Ippei hurriedly donned his gown and sat upright that brought to mind the behavior of a comic strip character and was the only flaw in the sequence of actions; even Ippei seemed to be aware that in that instant Kōji considered it so. For in thrusting his arm into the sleeve of the gown, while he hadn't actually committed the blunder of missing the opening completely, the action was certainly performed with a little too much haste.

Having entered that silk labyrinth, Ippei's emaciated, white, forty-year-old arm had thrashed about inside two or three times and, after struggling each time against the irresolute, unkind silk resistance of the lining cloth, had, at length, succeeded in grasping the awaiting air on its way out. There were certainly elements at work within this behavior that, had it continued even a fraction longer, would have upset the completion of this tableau vivant, but Ippei, when all was said and done, managed to exercise a modicum of subtle restraint.

The foursome, motionless, stared at one another. The act of looking seemingly transformed the person being looked at into some kind of monster. Like the chairman of a meeting, Ippei probably felt obliged to be the first to break the silence, and he spoke to Kōji. As far as Ippei was concerned, it was very fortunate that Kōji was there.

"Ah, I see you have come along as well. You've well and truly searched us out, haven't you? Madam is no doubt grateful to you."

Kōji sensed that this indirect form of address "Madam" had hurt Yūko terribly.

But, more than that, he felt bitterly disappointed and even betrayed. For at the moment Yūko appeared, Ippei failed to express intense delight or anything remotely resembling it. He thought about what had happened. *Wasn't it just such an expression of delight I had truly wanted to see? If it were not so, how have I endured six months of so much self-renunciation and humiliation?*

Had not Kōji desired to witness the very instant when the truth of perverse human nature begins to shine? The moment when a fake jewel emits the luster of the genuine article? Sheer delight itself? The manifestation of an irrational dream? The very moment when the ridiculous becomes the sublime? Kōji had loved Yūko out of such expectations; he had hoped to shatter the reality of her protected world, and he had even been prepared to accept that the consequences might ultimately lead to Ippei's happiness.

He would have at least rendered his services for the sake of somebody.

Whereas, what he had actually witnessed was nothing other than things he had grown utterly tired of seeing: the mediocre concealment of human shame, the irony of keeping up appearances. He had unexpectedly witnessed the ungraceful collapse of the drama he had believed in. The wind having been taken out of his sails, Kōji thought to himself, *If that's how it is, then it can't be helped. If nobody can change it, then by this hand I . . .*

But he didn't know how to change it, and he steadily felt himself losing his composure.

Yūko spoke with an enervated, hoarse voice. "Why don't you return home quietly, dear?"

Those words sounded awfully deflated, and Kōji wondered whether she hadn't lost her mind. Ippei extricated his legs from where he had thrust them under the quilt. He moved them as though he were swimming, fishing around on the floor for his slippers with those hirsute, white, spindly limbs, and having located them, he arranged his gown and sat upright on the bed. He began to talk in a tone of soft persuasion, but the import was quite the opposite.

"Come now, displaying that kind of attitude and telling me to go home will produce nothing but the opposite effect, don't you think? It's a foolish thing to say and doesn't become you at all. And as for myself, I shall return home when I consider it fit to do so and not when instructed to do so by my wife. Bringing matters to a conclusion at the eleventh hour is not a good idea. Now, darling, you run along first with Kōji here, and I will join you later. I trust there are no objections? I must also consider the position of this lady."

Just then, Kōji noticed Machiko quivering all over like a dog that, having returned home through the rain, suddenly vigorously shook off all the raindrops. And yet for all that, her pale made-up face remained completely expressionless.

But then Yūko dropped her parasol to the floor, and Kōji was startled as she covered her face with her hands and began to cry. It was a bitter, coarse, primitive cry, and one that he had no reason to have heard from her before. She slumped to her knees, still crying, and gave vent to a ceaseless torrent of indistinct utterances. How Ippei had hurt her despite her love, how she had persevered against these hardships, and how she had been waiting in the hope that his heart would return to her. This indulgent whining carried around the room in every direction as it left Yūko's body—which now lay crumpled on the carpet. It were as if dirty water was splashing through the air from a broken vase that had been dropped on the floor, and listening to this torrent Kōji wanted to cover up his ears—in the end, he screamed out in his mind: *Hurry up and die! Please let this woman die quickly!*

He may have hated Yūko, but, losing his presence of mind, his heart felt overwhelmed with sadness.

He became confused, so that he wasn't sure whom he hated. He felt miserable, as though he were being ignored—like a slender pencil barely managing to stand on end.

The three stood idly by for what seemed like quite some time, gazing at Yūko's crouching figure. Machiko stood up and made as if to help Yūko to her feet, and as she did so, Kōji saw how she was pulled up short by a look in Ippei's eye. That momentary failed action appeared meaningless and transparent, as if watching sand crumble and fall to pieces as it rises up from the seabed. Kōji wondered why it was that human beings occasionally make such strange gestures. It was the same type of behavior a bird exhibits when, perched on top of an unstable branch, it suddenly stretches up tall and then retracts its neck.

In any case, it wasn't of any great significance. Yūko continued crying and jabbering. Despite the rotating electric fan, the room, with its closed curtains, was grossly hot. At length, she stood up, the hem of her skirt in disarray, and rushed toward Ippei, appearing to leap on top of his knees, screaming as she went, "Go home! Go home right away!"

That she appeared to have leapt onto her husband's knees may have been due to the exaggerated impression they made at that moment, and maybe Yūko had only placed her tear-soaked, slack hand on the knees of Ippei's gown. Nevertheless, the upper half of Ippei's body collapsed backward on the bed; then, having gained momentum, it bounced back, pushing Yūko's bent body aside. More so than Machiko, it was possible that the presence of Kōji had been responsible for the strange vanity evident in that instant in Ippei's unnecessarily violent behavior. Perhaps, having brushed her aside, in that moment, Ippei had grabbed hold of his wife around the chest in an attempt to impart a life lesson to Kōji and in the hope of seeing society's distant approbation reflected in the younger man's eyes. Gripping her so, he struck his wife heavily across the cheek. Having been hit, Yūko was quiet, but Machiko uttered a slight shriek.

Bull's-eye! thought Kōji, looking on. Ippei had done her over pretty well. But far from deriving a cold sense of satisfaction, Kōji felt his whole body seething with excitement. Ippei struck Yūko once again. Her white face appeared docile like that of a doll, and with his arm no longer in place to support her, she collapsed obliquely onto the floor. Kōji reached into the inside pocket of his jacket. He later recalled the natural smoothness of his actions at that time. Without any hint of emotion, objective, or motive, he took part in a flowing series of spontaneous movements and, with no impediments, freely crossed the boundary of no return. Ippei turned his head. Kōji pounced and struck frenzied blows with the wrench he had clasped in his hand. The wrench buried itself terribly deeply, and Ippei's head moved in accordance with its impact.

Chapter 3

Meeting Ippei for the first time in two years, Kōji found him-self gazing at the head he had once struck with the wrench. The area had since been covered over with a thick growth of hair and was hidden from sight. Despite being exposed to the relentless glare of the sun, Ippei's hair did not shine.

As he was gazing intently, many impulsive recollections and ambivalent thoughts crowded Kōji's mind and blocked his vision, almost as if in the midst of the sunlight a drift-ing column of mosquitoes had suddenly and importunately obstructed his view.

At the time, I could no longer endure that putrid world; a world bereft of logic. It was necessary that I impart some logic into that world of pigs' entrails. And so you see, I imparted the cold, hard, black logic of iron. Namely, the logic of the wrench.

And again, *Yūko said herself in the bar that night,* "Seeing his impassive face, well, it would simply be the end." *Thanks to that attack, I've saved them both from that end.*

Then, aghast at such thoughts, *I have repented, I . . .*

The mosquito-like cloud of thoughts disappeared from before his eyes in an instant.

Kōji had already been informed during the course of the investigation:

The wrench blows, delivered to the left side of the head, had caused a collapsed fracture of the cranium and cerebral contusion. Even after Ippei had regained consciousness, the right side of his body was paralyzed, and aphasia was diagnosed.

Ah! And not forgetting the wrench. What a lot of troublesome, repetitive inquiry.

Machiko testified that it hadn't been in the room. The wrench bore the stamp of an electrical company, and its owner was traced. He had been to T Hospital by car, and while the wrench definitely belonged to his company, he claimed he had no recollection of dropping it. Furthermore, his car had not broken down once in the preceding month. In any case, whether it was stolen from some other place, or had been picked up from the ground, the wrench proved indelibly the premeditated nature of Kōji's crime. He was sentenced to seventeen months' imprisonment for bodily injury.

Ippei smiled from the shadow of the climbing roses as he laboriously guided them through the gate; the large white all-season blooming flowers around the trellised archway basked fully in the summer sun.

Kōji found it difficult to accept that anybody could change so much in such a short time. There no longer existed the dandy clothed in a finely tailored new suit, Italian silk shirt and tie, and sporting amethyst cuff links that sparkled somberly at his sleeves, who, the more he busily conducted himself in his daily affairs, created a more languorous atmosphere around himself. Kōji was horrified to think that all these changes had been brought about by a single attack.

In looking at Ippei and the result of the crime he had committed, Kōji felt as he imagined one would at seeing an illegitimate child several years after he had brought it into the world by way of a casual relationship. Of seeing the shadow of his own self seeping from the child. Ippei, as he was, was dead and gone, and in his place stood a deep shadow of Kōji's existence (of course, Ippei's face bore no resemblance whatso-ever to Kōji's). It was a human form that, rather than being a likeness of Kōji, resembled the form of the crime he had committed. If Kōji could sketch a self-portrait of his inner self, then Ippei would surely be the exact form it would take. Even the troubled look that cloaked Ippei's helplessly smiling countenance was, in truth, something that belonged to Kōji.

A recollection came suddenly to mind: Kōji remembered how he had once seen Ippei at the shop change into his din-ner jacket, insert a white rose in the buttonhole of his collar, and leave for a gamblers' party. It had been an elegant white rose that hung from his lapel. The same rose as those flowers that now threw shadows across Ippei's cheek. To make matters worse, the Ippei before him was slovenly dressed; the hemline of his gown did not meet, with the back of the garment askew and the dappled sash having slipped down loosely about the hips. The roses looked like ridiculous large white ornamen-tal hairpins as Ippei wound his way in and out of a festival procession.

"It's Kōji, you remember, don't you? Kōji."

Yūko slowly and clearly pronounced his name, and Ippei, still smiling that twisted smile, said, "Kooo . . . ri."

"Not Kooo . . . ri, Kōji."

Ippei continued. "Kooo . . . ri," and then, quite clearly, "how do you do?"

"It's strange, isn't it? The way he can say 'how do you do' without a hitch. It's not Kooo . . . ri. It's Kōji . . ."

Kōji became irritable and cut in. "It's all right. 'Kooo . . . ri' is okay. In fact, it suits me better. It's fine."

With greetings thus exchanged, their "first" meeting came to an end.

Kōji's irritation was complex; there was some impediment, and he was nettled by his inability to feel any regret. His whole being ought to have been a receptacle filled with remorse. Even before he saw Ippei's completely changed form, he ought to have dropped to his knees in tears and apologized. Instead, something had intervened, clogging the machinery and stopping this course of events. He couldn't put his finger on what it was; perhaps it was that unsettling smile that hung about Ippei's mouth like a spiderweb.

From a nearby branch, a summer bush warbler sang out, the sound blending with the chirring of cicadas. They went on through the rose gate, crossed the uneven flagstones, and passed alongside the greenhouses. Seeing Ippei's limping form, Kōji proffered a helping hand, but his action was cut short by Yūko's large, dark, expressionless eyes. Kōji didn't know why she had checked him. Perhaps she was trying to encourage Ippei to be more independent. In any case, he felt his deliberate gesture had been perceived, and he was hurt by her intervention.

"I'll show you around the greenhouses first. I've done it all myself. The research, the planning. I've built the place up and

I run it. It's developed into quite a business. For old acquaintance's sake, Tokyo Horticulture provides good trade with me. You wouldn't have imagined me capable of this in the past, would you? A woman, you see, has after all a considerable number of hidden talents. I'm quite impressed with it, if I do say so myself."

It wasn't clear how much of this rapid conversation Ippei was able to follow, although there was certainly a sense that part of what Yūko was saying to Kōji was for Ippei's benefit. That had been the case particularly since they passed through the rose-festooned archway. In fact, it had been that way even when Ippei was not close by—for example, even while they were on their way up from the harbor earlier—and, thinking about it, that was even the way it had been two years ago, before the incident.

A water pipe stood at the entrance to the greenhouse. Kōji abruptly turned on the tap and cocked his head obliquely to one side, drinking deeply of the gushing liquid. The force of the water as it spurted onto his cheek was pleasant. His face was exposed for a moment to this glistening collision and his pallid Adam's apple, which hadn't seen the sun for some time, moved feverishly as he drank.

"He certainly looks like he's enjoying that water."

"Wa . . . ter," said Ippei, echoing Yūko. Pleased that he had been able to say it so well, he repeated it. "Wa . . . ter."

Kōji looked up. In the entrance to the greenhouse stood a muscular old man wearing shorts and a running shirt. It was Teijirō, the gardener. He used to be a fisherman, and as Yūko had explained, he had a daughter who worked at the Imperial Instruments factory in Hamamatsu. Kōji was momentarily uneasy—maybe Teijirō knew where he had come from. But his anxiety was dispelled by Teijirō's firm, sun-weathered features—which resembled an ancient suit of armor—that looked out at him from under a closely cropped head of salt-white hair.

His face is not at any rate that of a person who tries to delve into others' affairs. Rather, it's like a closed window that he sometimes opens, just wide enough to allow the sunlight to filter through. He had known an old and sincere inmate with a similar face.

The four of them entered the first of five greenhouses. It contained mainly gloxinia and lady palm and so the three-quarter-span glass roof, which was built on a slope, was liberally screened with reed blinds. The violet, crimson, and white gloxinia compensated for the dull interior.

Kōji had learned to think about the beauty of flowers while in prison. But it had never transcended a mere sentimental appreciation from being continually near to them, so wasn't the sort of knowledge that would stand him in good stead in the future. Kōji was surprised by Yūko's loquacious explanation. This was clearly knowledge she had acquired in order to earn a living and, as such, far surpassed the fantasies of the likes of Kōji and his former fellow inmates.

Just then, they noticed a large black shadow fall suddenly across the sunlight that shone down on the flowers and leaves from the reed blinds above. Yūko had been boasting about the large blooms of her white gloxinia, and since the flower heads had darkened, everyone peered up toward the roof. With youthful agility, Teijirō ran along the narrow passageway between the flowers and foliage (Kōji quietly acknowledging Teijirō's ability to delicately pick his way through the undergrowth without so much as brushing the hard leaf tips of the lady palm that spread out all around), and rushed out in the direction of the entrance. They heard Teijirō yelling from outside, and then, like something that had suddenly exploded having been suppressed in the quiet sunlight, the shrieks and laughter of a group of mischievous youngsters erupted all at once and then subsided.

"This happens a lot. I wonder what they threw this time?"

Yūko looked up at the shadow, visible between the gaps in the reed blind; Kōji and Ippei followed her gaze. Strands of glittering sunlight were finely woven in the fabric of the blind, and Kōji vividly felt its origin all the more—the sun's penetrating rays. The shadow appeared large and ominous, but in fact the object that had been thrown was not so big at all. On the end of something that seemed to be covered in wet black hair was a long and thin hanging tail. It had to be a rat. The children must have found its remains and hurled them onto the roof. For some reason Kōji looked at Ippei's face. The face of the man whom Yūko had described on their way over here as a person who was unable to communicate freely his desires but whose spirit was immutable. That simple smiling face— a burial marker indicating the place where Ippei's spirit lived on, albeit incarcerated in a grave.

The shadow of the reed blind fell on his face and on Yūko's lips, and like a dark birthmark the shape of the dead rat appeared imprinted on Ippei's forehead. Then, suddenly, Teijirō's bamboo pole extended over the blinds, the rat was caught by the tip of the pole, and its shadow jumped skyward. It was hoisted higher and higher, ever closer to the sun, until in an instant it had become parched in its rays.

Soon the rainy season came. On the whole, it was unusually dry. In between the wet days, there were several of brilliant sunshine. On one such day, Yūko, Ippei, and Kōji went on a picnic to the great waterfall on the far side of the mountain.

Since Kōji's arrival some three weeks earlier, it appeared as if everything was going smoothly and their lives were settling into a new pattern. He had been provided with an airy six-tatami-mat room on the second floor, and, his daily schedule having been decided quickly, he became friendly with Teijirō. Kōji was given the important tasks of irrigation and the twice-daily spraying of plants—in the morning and evening. He worked hard, was well behaved, and exhibited a keen desire to learn, and before long he became popular with the local villagers who came to and fro.

Kōji laughed at the thought of how high-strung he had been when he had first arrived. He had repented, he was a different person from his former self, and he no longer had any concerns. He slept well at night, his appetite had improved, he was tanned, and before long, he was able to boast a healthy physique that compared favorably with the young men of the village. His daily independence was a pure delight, and he enjoyed the boundless freedom of strolling alone after work. Even on rainy days, he would set out on a walk, umbrella in hand, and soon he felt well acquainted with every corner of Iro Village. Yūko introduced Kōji to the chief priest of Taisenji temple, from whom he learned the topography and history of the surrounding area. At the close of the sixteenth century, the village formed part of the territory belonging to the local magistrate of Mishima but had, by the end of the Tokugawa Shogunate, come under the authority of the fiefdom of Mondo Manabe. Then, during the Meiji Restoration, it fell under the jurisdiction of Nirayama Prefecture together with many other scenic villages along the Izu Peninsula.

Yūko had taken up residence here via the good graces of the

head of Tokyo Horticulture, and having bought a house from one of the well-to-do villagers, she refurbished it and then erected five greenhouses on the grounds.

Yūko's ability, evidenced both in the administration of her disabled husband's estate and in her swift lifestyle transformation, was a source of wonder to those who had known her in the past.

And while Kōji wasn't so surprised to hear about her success, he was nevertheless increasingly astonished by Ippei's eccentric behavior. Ippei continued his habit of reading the morning newspaper, despite not understanding anything of what he read. He simply sat in silence, with the paper fully open so that the morning sun filtered through its pages. He would just move his head lightly up and down while maintaining this posture for quite some time.

On other occasions he would have Yūko bring him copies of his own literary works. Stefan George's collection of translated poems was tastefully bound in marbled German paper, while his critical biography of Li He was covered in an opaque yellow with a marbled ink drawing of a small bird on the inside cover. Sitting in front of his desk, he would fan himself with his left hand while repeatedly turning the pages with his lame right. Sometimes his fingers would get caught and the pages wouldn't turn over properly. Ippei, however, was undeterred.

Kōji had quietly watched Ippei from the side window of the greenhouse on the other side of the small garden. What a strangely detestable endeavor it was! If it was true that Ippei's spirit had not been laid to waste, then his inner spirit ought to have been in complete accord with his external literary works. Undoubtedly, George and Li He still lived on within Ippei's inner self. In spite of this, however, his view was obstructed by an invisible and impregnable wall, and he could neither

read nor comprehend his own writings. Kōji knew how he
felt. While in prison he had experienced the same longing for
the outside world—his frequent calls having fallen on deaf
ears. He felt that he understood Ippei better now than at any
time before.

He wondered what had become of Ippei's spirit. At first it
had probably been surprised at its own inability to understand
anything or express itself in words, and then, having eventually grown tired of exhibiting such surprise, had transformed
itself into another intelligent self that could do nothing other
than watch intently from the sidelines. His hands and feet
were bound and his intellect gagged; his literary works were
adrift, even now glittering in the distance, moving beyond his
reach and summons in the current of some dark and obscure
river. In a sense, it was as if the connection between spirit and
action had been severed and the one jewel that had been both
the source of his self-confidence and the measure of his public respect had split and become two complementary jewels,
which had then been placed on opposite banks of that large
dark river. And while the jewel on the far bank, namely his
literary works, was to the public at large the real treasure, to
Ippei, it was nothing more than a pile of rubble. Conversely,
while in the eyes of the general public the jewel on the near
bank, namely his spirit, had already turned to rubble, it was
to Ippei alone the only genuine jewel in his crown.

Furthermore, Ippei—that is, Ippei as he was before the
incident—had never attempted to conceal the cultivated man's
cold contempt for the generality of intellectual activities
(including in relation to his own literary works). In fact, wasn't
it his own psychological ruin that Ippei longed to achieve
through Kōji, rather than the bringing about of some sense
of mental cohesion? And that, too, was an artificial, affected,

and delicately engineered ruin. Little wonder then that Ippei's interminably meek smile provided a fresh source of astonishment for Kōji. The chief priest of Taisenji temple maintained that this was the manifestation of Ippei's spiritual enlightenment. Yūko, on the other hand, preferred to remain silent on the matter.

Oftentimes, the doctor asked Yūko, "Does your husband sometimes become really irritated? Does he ever give you a difficult time, or annoy you with his own selfishness?"

The doctor had always greeted Yūko's negative replies with a genuine look of suspicion. Those kinds of patients were extremely few and far between. Ippei had become quiet and tolerant, he accepted reality as it was, and he answered everything with the same warm, helpless smile.

Occasionally Kōji would feel unsettled by his smile—constantly and openly conveying as it did Ippei's sudden loss of hope. Ippei, who in the past had stood head and shoulders above Kōji in terms of his fun-loving ability, now appeared to have outstripped Kōji once more by his uncanny ability to accept his abandonment with such fortitude.

And what of Yūko?

Yūko once asked Kōji to bring some talcum powder to the bathroom. She had opened the badly creaking glass door of the dimly lit bathroom a fraction and called Kōji in from where he was in the sitting room. "Kōji! Kōji! I've run out of talcum powder—there's a new can on the top shelf of the closet. Be a darling and bring it in, would you?"

Possibly owing to the tastes of the house's former owner, the family bathroom was unusually spacious. The bathing area alone was some eight tatami mats in size, and added to this was a three-mat changing room.

Kōji had been reluctant to open the glass door, but Yūko

had spoken from inside. "It's all right—you can come in. I don't mind."

As Kōji suspected, Yūko, having bathed, had already changed into a neatly fitting large-patterned cotton *yukata*, held at the waist by a dark green Hakata-style sash. The upswept hairs on the nape of her neck were moist from the bath steam, and in the dusky light, beads of perspiration glistened alluringly on the surface of her rich skin like evening dew. Kōji recalled the sound of the driving, sultry rain as it pelted the roofs of the greenhouses in the early evening. He saw something strange at Yūko's feet as she sat there. In the gloomy light, the emaciated body of a naked man lay corpselike on its side, with closed eyes facing toward the ceiling and its lower half covered in white powder.

Kōji handed the new can of talcum powder to Yūko, and just as he started to leave, she called him back. "Oh! You are having a bath, aren't you? It's a waste of fuel not to use the water. Come on, the water's lovely and warm."

Kōji hovered in the open doorway.

"Come on in and close the door quickly; he'll catch his death in this draft. Relax—get undressed and get in."

A heap of powder that had already been sprinkled from the new container decorated the palm of Yūko's hand as she spoke. In the dull light it emitted a somber whiteness, like a poisonous drug. Kōji quickly undressed in a corner of the changing room. The door to the bathroom had been left ajar, probably in order to draw in the warmth produced by the steam, and so he left it open. While he bathed, his attention was drawn in the direction of the changing room. He felt the need for strangely oppressive, solitary, silent bathing, more so even than when he was in prison. There are certainly a great many bizarre rituals in the human world (all of which have been born of necessity)!

Yūko sprinkled the remainder of the white powder all over Ippei's bathed and naked outstretched body, painstakingly and affectionately massaging it in.

From time to time, her white fingers became visible here and there amid the dark billowing steam; vying with one another at sharp, almost reproachful angles, then continuing their movement in a more languid, hesitant manner.

Kōji, who had been watching all this from diagonally across the bathtub, suddenly felt a pang of excitement. He had imagined that his body was being caressed all over by those fingers. In reality, however, the flesh that Yūko's fingers massaged was enveloped in a frigidly indifferent and peacefully warm veil of death. There was no doubt about that. Even from this oblique angle, Kōji was certain of it. Having diligently washed in between Ippei's toes, Yūko next sprinkled on the white powder and enthusiastically rubbed it in. Now and again her beautiful profile revealed itself clearly through the steam. Her face was aglow, showing a kind of relaxed, self-indulgent pleasure, notwithstanding her fervor, and it appeared that Yūko's mind had found spiritual repose in this simple chore that produced both subservience and a sense of superiority. Kōji felt as though he was watching the sleeping form of her unchaste soul. He closed his eyes tightly in the bathtub.

Whether or not she had noticed Kōji's behavior, for the first time Yūko began talking to him in a cheerful, matter-of-fact tone. "I forgot to ask, but you sent your notice of withdrawal to the university, didn't you?"

"Yeah. I sent it from prison," he replied, splashing water noisily.

"That's a little rash, don't you think? Do you intend to bury your whole life in the Kusakado greenhouse?"

Kōji remained silent in the unpleasantly hot, dark bath-

water. He gazed at a strand of Yūko's long, shedded hair as it
formed a ring on the surface of the water. He pushed himself
out toward it, scooping it up with his wet chest.

And then came the picnic at the great waterfall. It had been the
cause of indecision for the past three weeks. Kōji had no idea
why it had been an issue. It certainly didn't seem as if Ippei
had anything to do with it. Kōji knew that Yūko wished for
the three of them to go together, and so he made a point of not
going to the waterfall during his leisure-time strolls. Then on
one particular clear and cool morning, it was suddenly decided
that they should set off on a picnic. There were no suitable
flowers in the greenhouse to offer to the waterfall shrine. So
Yūko had Kōji pick an especially large, single-flowered mountain lily from the cliff behind, and then she wrapped aluminum
foil around the base of its stem.

Yūko was wearing a Java calico blouse and yellow slacks
and, because of the rocky mountain paths ahead, had on a
pair of flat-heeled Moroccan leather walking shoes. Ippei was
in a state of disarray. He was attired in a white open-collared
shirt and knickerbockers, checkered socks and slip-ons and a
large straw hat. At his side he carried a stout stick. Naturally
Kōji, who wore jeans and a white shirt with the sleeves rolled
up, carried the camera and the basket containing their lunch
boxes and tea flasks. At normal walking speed, it ought to have
taken them about thirty minutes to the waterfall, but going at
Ippei's pace, Kōji estimated it would take at least an hour. In
the end, it took some two hours.

Yūko accompanied Ippei out of the gate and down the hill.
From here, there was a good view of the port. There was only
one boat lying at anchor. The green hills on the far side of the

bay were reflected on the surface of the tranquil body of water, projecting a shape like a draftsman's curve dissolving into the sea. There were a number of pearl divers' rafts; toward the back of one small inlet, the blue hull of a scrapped vessel lay half-submerged—listing as it had done when Yūko had first come to these parts. And silver oil tanks. A chorus of cicadas sang out; a small village crouched below them, and in the distance, a cloud of dust kicked up by a bus as it traveled along the prefectural highway quickly enveloped a whole block of shops—the barber's, the general store, the haberdashery, the drugstore, the confectioner's, and the *geta* store. The lighthouse at the bay entrance, the ice-crushing tower, and the village lookout tower, being the three tallest buildings, lorded it over the even rows of houses. To the east all they could see were the gently sloping mountains that they would soon climb. The trees and the grass had begun to dry out from the morning dew and the previous day's rain. The rising water vapor and sunlight appeared to completely cover the surface of the mountains and forests in trembling silver leaf. It was extremely quiet, so much so that it seemed as if the mountains and forests were lightly enveloped in some sort of glittering shroud of death.

From far in the distance they could hear the sound of a quarry compressor.

"That's the route we're taking. You can see it, can't you? The path follows the river winding its way up through the mountains."

Yūko indicated the way with the single-flowered lily she was carrying. The lily extended its glossy white petals as if they were coated in oil and gave out a melancholy fragrance under the strong summer sun. It was messily dyed with brick-colored pollen right up to the edges of its white petals. The inside—all the way deep down—was buff-colored with brilliant dark red spots. The stem that supported this heavy flower was strong and gave it a neat and dignified appearance.

As if by magic, the landscape took on the elegant shape of the lily. The mountains and the clear sky and the glistening clouds above them now came under the control of this single flower. Each and every color appeared to be diffused, having been condensed into the color of the lily. It was as if the green of the forest was the color of the lily's stem and leaves; the earth, the color of its pollen; the trunks of the ancient trees, the color of its dark red spots; the glistening clouds, the color of its white petals . . .

Kōji's heart was inexplicably filled with joy. This was the happy recompense of repentance, the kind of happiness that comes after a period of abandonment. After two years of anguish, each of them had, perhaps, finally found happiness— Yūko had Ippei exactly as she wanted him, Kōji had his freedom, and, as for Ippei, he had something very peculiar.

Suddenly a kite cried out high above them.

"Teijirō told me he can tell how the weather will change by listening to the birds," said Kōji. "He can read the weather signs—like from a red sky in the morning or from a halo around the moon or the sun. I know that's pretty common, but he can also tell the weather from the birds singing and even from the light of the stars."

"I've never heard of anything like that before," said Yūko. "Where is Teijirō, anyway?"

"He was in the greenhouse earlier," replied Kōji.

"I see. Hmm . . . is that right?" said Ippei.

But it was too much trouble to turn back simply to inquire about the weather, and instead they began to descend the slope. As they walked along, Kōji was again overcome with thoughts of happiness. They came upon him from behind and persistently hung about him, the way a child clings to its parent's neck. *How could we possibly have had such a happy and peaceful moment as this before the incident?* he continually thought. *Certainly when Yūko came to meet me at the harbor, and even during our conversation at the grassy knoll at the rear of the bay, she had seemed no different at all than before. But that was probably the result of her hiding her feelings of happiness out of consideration for me after my release from prison. Maybe it was this that she really wanted to show me. Perhaps that was the real reason why she went out of her way to invite me to Iro in the first place. If that is the case,* thought Kōji in sudden realization, *then this happiness has undoubtedly been brought about by that single attack with the wrench.*

At length the slope leveled out, and below them they could see the back garden of Taisenji temple and part of the priest's living quarters. In the temple garden, a large number of droning honeybees hovered around a pomegranate tree that was festooned with scarlet flowers and a camellia with shiny leaves. One of the bees, having separated from the swarm, flew loftily toward them and landed on Ippei's straw hat. Kōji borrowed Ippei's walking stick and deftly knocked the bee to the ground. This was the second time he had raised his hand to Ippei's head. The three of them smiled at this little triumph, and that, more than anything, provided comforting proof that no one associated Kōji's actions with past events.

The smitten bee lay dust-covered on the road, buzzing quietly.

"The priest will be angry with you," said Yūko.

The priest, Kakujin, kept the wild honeybees. He had set up a hive beneath the floor and, from time to time, collected

the honey to spread on his toast at breakfast. As if he had heard
their conversation, the priest, who had been sitting at the back
of his quarters, slipped on his *geta* and came down and stood
in the back garden. Kakujin was shaven-headed with a healthy
complexion and round face; he was in every detail exactly as
one would imagine a chief priest. His face was a moderate
mix of the secular and the transcendent with no trace of cold-
ness whatsoever. He was, so to speak, a small, living portrait
of the archetypal chief priest of a parish temple in a fishing
village.

Yūko had already discussed the matter with Kōji, and it
had been apparent from their first meeting that the priest considered them to be different from the run-of-the-mill sort of
people he usually came into contact with. And because of this,
the priest, too, had behaved in a way that made him stand out
from that small portrait. This was painful for Yūko and Kōji.
They had both been terribly fond of the priest's small portrait
and had even wanted to be included in a corner of it. The priest
had lived in this peaceful village for a long time, and it was
evident that he thirsted after people's suffering. Of course, Iro
had seen a lot of unhappiness: death, old age, sickness, pov-
erty, domestic trouble, the sadness of parents with disabled
children born of incestuous marriage, shipwrecked fishermen,
the grief of the bereaved family left behind. However, in this
countryside region, there was no "Great Doubt" of the sort
encountered by Master Bankei when he was twelve or thirteen
years old. In this village, there was none of that particular
type of spiritual awakening—that craving for "seeing one's
true nature"—so characteristic of the Rinzai school of Zen.

It seemed the priest had been casting his net out for a considerable time—trying for a good catch. But for many years
now the spiritual yield had been poor. When Yūko first came

to the village and introduced herself, the priest must have sniffed out in this seemingly lively and cheerful, handsome-faced city girl the prey he had long been searching for. It was the smell of anguish, a smell that one with a nose for it could detect well in advance—a smell that Yūko herself had possibly not been aware of.

And what was more, this time, an unusually well-behaved, diffident, and hardworking young man had also come along—again, with that same smell. That delicious smell. There was no doubt that only the priest had detected it. He had been very kind to both Ippei and his wife and to Kōji, showing them warm friendship. It was a kindness born out of consideration for the delicious prey he had been craving for so long. All this was, of course, pure conjecture on the part of Yūko and Kōji. The priest had not once asked any probing questions; neither had Yūko nor Kōji volunteered information about their personal circumstances without being asked.

"Where are you all off to?" asked the priest in a loud voice from where he stood in the middle of the garden.

"For a picnic at the waterfall," replied Yūko.

"That will be hard work in this heat. Your husband will be all right, won't he?"

"He needs an outing to exercise his legs."

"Oh, that's extremely commendable. And, Kōji, I see you are the picnic bearer, aren't you?"

"Yeah," said Kōji, laughing, swinging the large picnic hamper up for him to see. In that instant his heart, which had until then been filled with happiness, clouded over at the sight of the priest's smiling face. Kōji recalled the reception he had received when, several days earlier, he had gone down to the village barber's and tobacconist.

When he entered the barber's shop, he had sensed that

the conversation between the barber and his customers had
abruptly come to an end, and while he was having his hair
cut, the shop was enveloped in an eerie silence, so that all he
could hear was the noise of scissors and clippers. And on the
way home, when he stopped off at the tobacconist, the shop
assistant's familiar face suddenly tightened when she laid eyes
on him. He had bought some cigarettes and then left. Behind
him, he heard the girl's feet kick off the tatami mats as she
turned and hurried toward the back of the shop.

Kōji sensed he had seen in the priest's carefree smile just now
the two different faces of the village's reaction to his presence.

"I'm tired. I'm tired," began Ippei as they approached the eastern fringes of the village, turned left in front of the local shrine,
and began at last to climb the mountain path.

With nothing else to do, they sat down on a rock in the
shade of a tree. Yūko had Kōji take a picture of her with Ippei,
and then she took one of Kōji and Ippei together. She was
uneasy about giving the camera to Ippei, and so there was no
picture of just her and Kōji.

When they were stuck for conversation, Kōji talked about
prison. Yūko would frown at this but Ippei, seemingly pleased
with the subject, leaned forward on his knees in an effort to
understand as much as possible. Kōji, solely for Ippei's benefit, slowly and concisely enunciated each and every word as
he spoke. During the conversation, Yūko carefully brushed off
an ant that had been crawling up Ippei's unmoving right leg.

Kōji took out a small comb from the back pocket of his
jeans, and with the light sifting down through the trees onto
its candy-colored mock tortoiseshell, he showed it to Ippei and
asked him what it was.

"Co . . . mb," replied Ippei, after a few seconds, extremely pleased with himself at seeing Kōji's acknowledgment.

Like a conjurer, Kōji turned the comb over and stroked its spine. "Can you see? It's not worn down at all, is it?"

Yūko, also interested, moved her face closer and gave off a whiff of the perfume she had applied to the base of her ears.

"The inmates' combs are all worn away here. In the worst cases, they are worn pretty much all the way down to the base of the teeth. And can you guess why? Well, I'll tell you—it's called 'gori.' What you do is you make a celluloid powder by rubbing the back of the comb on the windowpane in the toilets. Then you tightly wrap the powder in cotton, about the thickness of a cigarette, add a little tooth powder, and then rub it hard on a board until it ignites. You use it to light any cigarettes you manage to filch. If this gori is discovered, it's two weeks in solitary. There was a guy who used to sing 'Even without a match, a butt is lighted; distant yet so close, passions are ignited.'"

He lit his own cigarette, drew deeply on it, and narrowed his eyes.

"Does it taste good?" asked Yūko.

"Yeah, it's good," he replied, in a slightly ill-humored manner. It bothered him that cigarettes were no longer as good as they had been just before his release from prison.

Anyone looking at the garbage-filled river mouth by the wharf would find it hard to believe that this river had its origin in the great waterfall deep in the Taiya Mountains, hard to believe that it was the same as that limpid mountain stream water that seethed over the riverbed, sending spray over the moss-covered rocks.

They followed the mountain path—which could hardly be described as being very steep—upstream, and as they came to the top of the wide trail, the sunlight came through the trees and carried with it on the wind the chirring of cicadas, as if the dappled sunlight itself was in full chorus. And then they were in the pleasantly cool deep shade of a clump of cedar trees.

"I'm tired," repeated Ippei.

By the time they reached the waterfall, they had taken four long impromptu breaks, and although they had planned to eat lunch at the plunge pool below the waterfall, they had polished off their lunch boxes at the third stop, on account of Kōji constantly complaining that he was hungry. That was already after noon. And, because each time they stopped to rest, Kōji always descended the valley to dip Yūko's mountain lily into the stream, so that it retained its beautiful fragrance and vigor.

The waterfall couldn't be much farther now.

Ippei clambered to his feet—signaling, in theatrical fashion, that they should start. Clearly he was aware that he was clowning around. He thrust forward his walking stick and knickerbocker-clad left leg—"Off we go!"—and then swung the whole of his body around from the right, lifting his right leg up like a heavy crane.

Yūko cheered him on.

"Off we go!"

Kōji tidied the picnic away, confident that he would soon be able to catch up to them no matter how far ahead they got, and gazed after their retreating forms as they appeared to dissolve into the hazy sunlight that sifted down through the trees onto the pebble path.

It was an absurd sight—Yūko doggedly echoing Ippei, "Off we go!"

Kōji was beguiled by that hollow voice, lost in the torrent

of the stream. He felt as though the predicament in which he had been placed was as heavy, cold, and immovable as stone. He lengthened the strap of the tea flask and slung it across his shoulder together with the camera and set off with a careless swing of the empty picnic basket.

Having crossed a moldering wooden bridge and climbed a roundabout set of stone steps, Yūko now stood in front of the small shrine, listening to the roar of the waterfall through the dense clump of cedar trees; there was a clear look of contempt in her eyes.

"It's a pretty dull, small shrine, isn't it? It's ridiculous to think we've carried the lily all this way to make an offering at a place like this. And what is this cheap muslin curtain with the rosette pattern supposed to mean?"

Inside the shrine, the flame of a candle that was about to expire flickered precariously, and several strings of paper cranes that had all but lost their color swayed ever so slightly in the updraft.

Kōji was afraid of Yūko's sacrilege.

It was a sacrilege without reason or motive—nothing other than a moody fixation with an illusion she had herself waywardly created.

"But the object of worship at this shrine is the waterfall itself, isn't it? Who cares about the cheap curtain?"

Yūko was annoyed about something. Her anger-filled eyes flashed as they caught the piercing rays of light coming over the cedar tops.

"All right, then we can throw the lily into the pool, can't we?"

Then they rested on an expansive sheet of rock at the side of the plunge pool. After hearing the roar of the waterfall, something had changed inside Yūko. She laughed wildly, and then just as suddenly fell silent. Her emotions were self-indulgent—her hot, moist eyes held the waterfall in their gaze, and her dark crimson lips, unsmiling, twisted every now and then.

The view of the waterfall was magnificent.

From a height of some two hundred feet the black rock summit shone in the brilliant light that was penetrating the disordered clouds above, and out from between the light-filled gaps in a sparse coppice water came skipping and jumping in short bursts before cascading downward. All they could see of the upper third was white spray, and while the rock surface wasn't visible, lower down the water divided itself in two and surged outward as if suddenly attacking the onlookers below. Finally, the flow formed a multitude of columns and then descended abruptly with a shake of its foaming white mane.

The only things growing on the rocks that agitated the water were a small number of weeds that were soaked right through to their stems.

The direction of the wind was constantly changing and one couldn't be certain from where the spray was next going to come. The sunlight leaking through the tall vegetation on the bank to the right was a picture of tranquility as it threw streaks of even, parallel light across the falling water. The air was filled with the sound of the waterfall and the chirring of cicadas. The two quarreled with each other and at times seemed like one and the same, and yet, at other times their sounds were quite distinct.

They lay down on the rock surface, each adopting a position according to their own fancy. Ippei had taken the lily from where it lay at Yūko's side and placed it over his face as he reclined on his back. It was difficult to interpret if Ippei's actions were deliberately exaggerated or if they had been abandoned in midflow. This time, it wasn't obvious whether he had been trying to appreciate the lily's fragrance or, perhaps, pretending to devour the flower.

At any rate, his distinguished nose and mouth had been buried in the lily for quite some time. The other two, their ears deafened by the thunder of the waterfall, were pretending not to have noticed.

Then suddenly Ippei began to choke violently and flung the flower away, leaving a startled face speckled around the tip of the nose and cheeks with brick-colored pollen. Or had he been trying to commit suicide with the flower?

Yūko propped herself up. She retrieved the slightly battered lily, took hold of the aluminum-wrapped stem base, and pensively waved it around casually several times in her red-nailed manicured fingers. This was the first time Kōji had seen such a lack of respect in her eyes as she regarded Ippei.

"Say, do you understand 'sacrifice'?"

She stared into Ippei's face as he lay once again on his back and posed the question in a contemptuous voice.

Ippei was surprised at the tone of his wife's question, which was clearly different than usual.

"Sacr . . . fish?"

"No, that's not right. Don't you understand the word 'sacrifice'?"

"I don't understand."

Kōji thought Yūko was being unduly hard on Ippei and so he interrupted. "It's too difficult for him, you know, such an abstract word."

"Be quiet. I'm testing him."

Turning her face to Kōji, she smiled in a relaxed, rather

vague manner instead of the harsh look that he had expected
to see.

Kōji stared at several stray hairs blown across Yūko's forehead by the wind from the waterfall and suddenly remembered
that single strand of hair floating in the dark bathtub.

"You must have some idea? You're an idiot, aren't you? This
is what I'm talking about."

Without warning, Yūko threw the lily she had been holding
into the plunge pool. The discarded flower formed a shining
white circle in front of them.

Dark confusion spread across Ippei's face. This was something else Kōji had not seen before—a look of pure anxiety
born of being cut off from all understanding.

Yūko was enjoying herself to the point where she couldn't
control herself any longer. She bent backward, choking back
tears of laughter, and then quickly asked, "How about the
word 'kiss,' then? Do you understand that?"

"Ki . . ."

"Try to say 'kiss.' "

"Ki . . ."

"You're stupid, aren't you? You don't understand, do you?
Well, I'll show you. It's like this."

She turned about and suddenly wrapped herself around
Kōji's neck as he was leaning forward. The rocks were slip-
pery, and Kōji was caught off guard by this surprise attack.
Yūko's lips pressed blindly against his, and their teeth bumped
together. After this collision came a meeting of the flesh. She
advanced and inserted her tongue into Kōji's mouth, and Kōji,
drawn into that warm, tender morass, swallowed her saliva.
His senses benumbed by the unceasing boom of the waterfall,
he couldn't tell how much time had passed. When their lips

parted, he was angry. He sensed that the kiss had, surely, been for Ippei's sake.

"Lay off, will you? Stop tormenting him like this for your own amusement."

"He isn't suffering."

"What would you know about that? In any case, I object to being used like this."

Yūko looked up at him mockingly. "What are you saying, after all this time? When you've been used from the very beginning. You like it, don't you?"

In spite of himself, Kōji struck Yūko across the cheek. He left his hand there and, without looking at her, turned to face Ippei.

In that instant, Ippei had an unmistakable smile on his face.

It was exactly the same smile—the embodiment of Ippei's new character—that Kōji had first seen following his release from prison, and for the first time he felt he understood what it meant. He had been rejected, forced out by that smile.

There was something about Ippei's smile that reminded him of that serene hourglass that had come and gone amid the billowing steam of the dirty prison bathhouse. Struck with fear, Kōji embraced Yūko. He gazed at her cold, meek face and her closed eyes as she lay in his arms. He kissed those lips, working in vain to rid his mind at once of the image of Ippei's smile. But this time the kiss had lost completely its exquisite taste.

When he came to, the sky had clouded over. Being unprepared for bad weather, they tidied their things away in silence, helped one another to their feet, and thought about the long and arduous trek home through the rain. Yūko carried the empty picnic hamper on the return journey.

Chapter 4

One particular evening after the end of the rainy season, Kōji found himself drinking alone in the only bar in the village. Lately, he had been coming here often on his own. The worse his estrangement from the villagers became, the more he came deliberately into the middle of the village to drink. And when the young villagers, who had returned in dribs and drabs at the end of the fishing season, heard the rumors about Kōji's prison record, this only served to heighten their curiosity and their desire to become his drinking companions. Kōji's crime became the relish for their beer—like a meritorious deed carried out on the field of battle in days gone by.

Even now, when he came down to the village from the Kusakado greenhouse, the sight of the star-filled midsummer night sky never ceased to amaze him. It was altogether different from the sky one saw in the city. Those innumerable stars were like a huge blanket of shiny mildew growing across the heavens.

It was a dark night in the village, with the brightest lights belonging to the last bus stopping at Toi at 8:45 p.m. and the occasional passing truck, their headlights shining mercilessly as they played on the rows of old houses standing alongside the prefectural highway.

The bus was supposed to run once an hour, but sometimes two or three came one after another in succession, or else nothing came along at all for two hours or more. Each time these large vehicles passed by, the rows of houses would vibrate like old chests of drawers, and then, when the bus stopped at the central crossroads and discharged its load of passengers, the local youths—who had been enjoying the cool of the evening on the roadside—teasingly greeted the familiar faces they recognized.

Even at night, there were a couple of fairly well-lit ice shops, with general menus displaying items like watermelons, lemonade, and Chinese noodles. They even had televisions, and the young villagers would congregate there to watch a baseball game or boxing match.

The bar, Storm Petrel, stood alone on the northern fringes of the run of stores, isolated from the others, and gave out all the more a dim light in the dark town. It was a crude hut with blue-painted panel walls; the sign, in English, should have displayed "Storm Petrel," but the painter had mistaken the spelling and instead it read "Storm Pertel."

But nobody criticized this oversight, and even the proprietor didn't mind, so the black lettering, which was now covered in dust from the passing buses, had soon taken on an aged appearance.

Several dozen empty beer bottles were piled up to one side

of the entrance. Despite the heat, the windows were closed in by crimson curtains.

Now and then, a popular song played in the background. The twenty-square-yard interior was bathed in a dim red light and looked a little shady. There was no barmaid, so the husband and wife proprietors had to take drinks orders themselves. There were just a few plain tables and chairs scattered about the room.

In one corner, a token stand-up bar had been installed, with an electric fan above it, and there was a tabby cat that, despite having its tail yanked constantly by the younger customers, only ever reacted by wearily changing its sleeping position.

It was early, and the regular customers hadn't yet gathered. Kōji swapped gossip about Teijirō's daughter, Kimi, with the owner. Kimi hadn't stayed with her father at all during her ten-day vacation from the instrument factory in Hamamatsu. She had stayed the first night in a room of her own at the Kusakado greenhouse, and after that she lodged at the Seitōkan—an inn owned by her relatives. Teijirō himself had hardly spoken a word to his daughter, despite her long absence.

It seemed there were some ill feelings between them that nobody had previously been aware of. They had lived together, quite happily on the face of it, for some time after her mother had died.

Then one day Kimi suddenly left home and went to work as a factory girl in Hamamatsu; her father closed up the house and went to live at the Kusakado greenhouse, where a gardener was needed. Since his arrival in the village, Kōji hadn't heard any stories about Teijirō's daughter from Teijirō himself.

Not only was Kimi beautiful but she also knew it, and she

let everyone else know it, too. The village girls and ordinary
locals considered her presence a nuisance.

Before Kimi came home, several girls would come along
with the local young men to drink at the Storm Petrel. But once
she returned, she became the only female customer in the place.

Before long, this otherwise reputable drinking establishment—
which had never before suffered any kind of moral censure—
came to be seen as a place of ill repute.

This sudden decline in reputation in a matter of a few days
was a remarkable change, and yet Kimi was not the sort of
woman to behave flirtatiously.

Matsukichi, a fisherman, and Kiyoshi, a member of the Self-
Defense Forces, both Kimi's childhood friends, quarreled over
her. But so far, there was no indication that she had given
herself to either of them.

Kimi owned a ukulele. She carried this brand-new item—
the manufacture of which she had been partly responsible for—
wherever she went. Occasionally, while drinking, she would
strum the instrument and sing. From deep within her bosom
(which was the largest among all the girls in the village), from
the bottom of the ashen gloom that drifted up from the flesh
of her breasts, her voice rose up like a bucket in a well, brimming with abundant quantities of water, and those around
soon forgot how poor her singing really was.

At around 9:00 p.m., Kimi, Matsukichi, and Kiyoshi came
into the bar together with three other youngsters, and with
their arrival, the peaceful evening in the Storm Petrel came
to an end.

Kiyoshi called over to Kōji, who moved away from the bar
and joined them at their table.

As usual, Kimi had her ukulele. The distant breeze from the electric fan blew her stray hairs about as she drank a highball and explained, in a businesslike manner, how the ukulele was manufactured.

First of all, the various parts are laid out in order: the mahogany sound board, the maple sides, and the neck. A groove is introduced into the sound board with a cutter and the circumference of the sound hole is then decorated with celluloid inlay. This was Kimi's job.

The sides of the gourd-shaped body were formed by boiling the wooden boards and then bending them into shape using an electric press mold.

There were also more intricate stages of the manufacturing process, such as attaching the linings and plastic bindings, and sanding the edges of the ukulele's body. But the task that demanded the highest degree of technical skill was attaching the neck to the body, and this was a job undertaken by fastidious craftsmen.

Once the rosewood fret board had been glued on, the instrument was polished with cloth before being sent to be lacquered. After the body assumes its perfectly polished finished form, four nylon strings are attached to complete the instrument— and the ukulele is ready to produce its first sound.

The sober luster of the dark mahogany instrument, which Kimi now held in her hands, appeared like restless agate or a drink-reddened chest in the red lighting. There was a sense of the carefree, like the firm flesh of a precocious girl, in the small gourd-shaped object. Its whole being seemed to have been designed in order to tease and cajole with its easy sound. Further still, stealing a look as far as one could inside the body of the instrument from the sound hole revealed a boundless, sweeping landscape of agitated shadows and shapes and dust-

choked nooks and crannies—like the backstage scene in some
grand theater. Kōji thought it amusing that Kimi had discovered an instrument so like herself in character.

Such a detailed explanation of the manufacturing process
suggested a strange detachment between Kimi and this instrument. While right now the instrument certainly belonged to
her, there would forever exist a tantalizing distance between
the hands that once helped create it in the wood shaving–filled
factory and the instrument itself.

Kōji found it easy to imagine the factory where Kimi worked.
The high steel ceilings, the roar of the various machines, scattered deposits of sawdust, the strong, invigorating smell of
lacquer . . .

At any rate, it would not be too dissimilar to the prison
paper factory where he had worked for fifty yen a month making a variety of multicolored supplements for sundry children's
magazines.

It was tough when the New Year's editions were due out.
There was the first supplement, and then the second, and by
the end of the season there would have been as many as five
printings.

How he had adored the colors—like the gaudy plumage
of a cockatoo! The supplements were full of paper handbags,
paper brooches, floral design paper clocks, self-assembly paper
furniture, paper pianos, paper flower baskets, and paper beauty
salons—all done out in festival colors and printed on glossy
paper.

If the print had shifted a little out of line, the effect produced an even more dazzling blaze of color.

One of the inmates who had children of his own had wept as
he made the paper products. But Kōji didn't have that prob-
lem. Yet when he imagined children receiving these toys and

the warmth and comfort of their homes, he felt more anguish than when he recalled neon-lit streets of bars.

One time, when he was walking around Numazu following his release from prison, he noticed a pile of beautiful children's magazines, stuffed full of supplements, heaped up under the protruding summer awning at the entrance to a bookstore. *Maybe I made one of those supplements*, he reflected as he glanced furtively at them.

He resolved never to have children. He wouldn't be able to bear watching his child delightedly fingering the paper toys. He felt sure he would be a hard-to-please, disagreeable father. Kōji wanted to distance himself forever from those supplements. To him they used to symbolize those who had colorful, festive lives and who enjoyed the pleasures of a happy home. But then the hands that had made these supplements were the same roughly cracked hands that had committed that crime . . .

All the while he was listening to Kimi's explanation, he kept thinking about the secret process for the production of the beautiful "special" children's supplements. Although Kimi's hands were not those of a criminal, the dismal nature of working in an instrument factory was not so far removed from his own experience.

And so he felt that, though she may not have been doing so deliberately, she was bragging about it shamelessly. At least that's how it seemed to him. Working amid the dust, the wood shavings, and the smell of lacquer, Kimi brought one of those beautiful completed products home as a keepsake. Still, Kōji found it hard to believe the way she finally was able to possess every single aspect of the finished ukulele—its perfect smoothness, carefree tunes, the lyricism of "South Island," and its leisurely melancholy . . . It was clearly "Kimi's ukulele," and it would remain distinct from the other thousands of ukuleles. By rights she herself ought never to have been able to acquire a real ukulele, the perfect instrument, and so it had become her icon.

The cat played around Kōji's feet. From time to time, it extended the claws of its forepaws slightly and raked playfully at his insteps where they were exposed between the thongs of his *geta*. Since it was summer, it didn't come onto the customers' knees, preferring instead to lie with its stomach on the cool concrete floor. The cat liked Kōji, but Kōji disliked this strange, unaccountable fondness. With the tip of his toe he lightly kicked the cat away. But it soon came back again. At the Kusakado greenhouse, they would sometimes use bonito stock as well as chemical fertilizer. But it didn't make Kōji reek of fish any more than the fishermen.

Kimi strummed her ukulele and sang a Hawaiian song she had picked up in the women's dormitory at the Hamamatsu factory.

She was wearing a black, sleeveless beach dress with a sunflower pattern. A shadow was cast vertically into the cleavage of her voluptuous breasts, incongruous against her small stature. On a mere whim, she had clean-shaven one of her armpits, but left some stubble on the other. Her slightly stern face wore a frown, her mouth was like a beautiful half-open sea cucumber, and her dark skin was deeply reddened—maybe from the drink or perhaps from the lighting in the bar.

Kiyoshi was listening intensely to her, his bright, round face nestled in the turned-up collar of his white aloha shirt. Matsukichi, who was wearing a cotton waistband rolled up above his chest, rested his elbow on the tabletop, his chin on his hand.

Kōji sat across the table gazing intently at this stiflingly hot, still scene, as if looking through a picture frame.

He thought about Yūko and suddenly felt choked with emotion. *I have repented, I have . . .* He hadn't realized before now just how much he was in love with her. If he were honest about it, he had to admit that he hadn't wielded that wrench for her. However, he was sure he was in love now.

The bitter taste of contrition heightened the sweetness of his desire, and his longing for Yūko made its presence known here and there on the most unexpected and delicate of occasions. Kōji now felt constantly afraid of being ambushed by such desires. Yūko's trifling gestures—the way she would raise her upper arm when she put a hand to her hair; the line of her skirt as she descended, in a stooped manner, the greenhouse steps; the fragrance of her face powder as it began to yield a little to the perspiration beneath . . . When these gestures suddenly shook him to his very foundations, he felt as though he had been waylaid by his own desires—stabbing him sharply in the back.

But the impossibility of the situation was even more apparent than before. Like living in a house built above a river with the constant clamor of water below, every inch of Kōji's desire was directly linked to the noise of a culvert flowing through the memory of that dark jail. *I have repented, I have . . .* Whenever his desire for something arose, it inevitably revived his crime. Whether or not she was aware of Kōji's feelings, Yūko had not allowed him to kiss her since the incident during the picnic.

Kōji scratched the bridge of his nose. It itched, unhappily, as if a fly were trying to scurry up his face.

It was clear from Yūko's expression that some kind of change had occurred inside her since the picnic. During the hot evenings, there were times when she would pant faintly through open lips. She would gaze, absentmindedly, at a fixed point, and sometimes she would address Kōji in an unfriendly manner and make stinging remarks. And what was more, she seemed scarcely aware of the changes that had occurred within herself.

"Would anyone like this ukulele?" asked Kimi suddenly, the high pitch of her inebriated voice bringing an end to Kōji's reverie. From around the table, the young men raised their big, rough hands. Kōji, too, extended his arm meekly. The ukulele, now held aloft in Kimi's grasp, shone in the red light, and looked like the rigid corpse of a waterbird being hoisted aloft by its neck. She toyed with the instrument's strings with her thumb, and those nearest the pegs gave out a solemn, dry noise.

"No, you don't! I won't give it away so easily, you know. This ukulele is my flesh and blood. When I give it to someone, I'm giving myself to them."

"So whoever gets your ukulele gets to be with you?" asked one of the young men, in an obtuse manner.

"Well, there's no guarantee of that."

"Still, I guess if we see a man walking around the village with your ukulele, that means he's the guy you're in love with, right?"

"Yes, that's right." Kimi brushed up a stray hair and answered decisively.

"Do you mean it? Will you swear on it?" said Matsukichi, speaking for the first time.

Kiyoshi gnawed at his nails in silence, his eyes glittering.

They were all drunk. They pressed Kimi to make a vow, and the proprietor was brought in to be a witness.

One of the young men scooped up the cat and placed it on the beer-stained table. The cat, with its sparse summer coat, squatted, pinioned by a hand on its back. Its bent body looked like it contained a strong but flexible spring, as if it were waiting for an opportunity to make a swift escape.

"Put your hand on the cat's back and swear. If you lie, then you'll turn into a cat, too."

"That's crazy!" exclaimed Kimi contemptuously, placing her hand on the back of the squirming animal and swearing an oath at the top of her voice. "There, I've done it. Now, let's go for a swim, shall we?"

"Is that a good idea after we've had so much to drink?"

"Call yourself a man? You coward. Come on—let's take a dip at Urayasu."

Kimi started to leave first and, carrying her ukulele, turned to face the others from the entrance to the bar and shouted, in a deliberately affected accent, "Come on. Let's go! Let's go!"

In the end, only Kiyoshi, Matsukichi, and Kōji decided to go with Kimi. The four of them sang raucously as they headed for the harbor. At the wharf, only the area in front of the refrigerated ice store was glaringly bright. The electric motor for the freezer in the ice plant hummed on late into the night. There were a few shadowy figures squatting along the seawall close by, fishing for horse mackerel.

They hadn't been down there for a while, and the number of ships alongside the wharf had increased considerably. The white underside of one ship appeared alternately bright and then dark again as the beam from the lighthouse near the bay entrance reached it. Similarly, the silver oil tanks standing on the opposite shore intermittently appeared small and white, and then disappeared from view again. Above this vantage point, countless stars filled the night sky.

Kōji thought again about Yūko. Even when he was apart from her for a moment, or perhaps because he was apart from her, his mind was continuously occupied by thoughts of her. A stern line groaned. One of the ships sulkily pulled on the rope, and then slowly pushed back and let it go slack again. He could only lament his bad fortune at running into this indescribably cold and evasive woman just as he was at last of the age to make a go of life. It was his fate. The world was full of young men who accepted their destinies lightly the way one wears a wristwatch, without much conscious thought. But his destiny was like a plaster cast.

He was so in love with her, and yet he suffered from the vague anguish of the moral impossibility of the situation and the fact that he was unable to capture her heart. Why now had Yūko summoned him to these parts?

If it was out of a sense of regret and atonement, then what did that kiss and the terrible things she said at the waterfall mean? In the end, thinking like this, his fondness for her only succeeded in raising doubts about what sort of person Yūko really was.

Kōji became alert as an unaccountable agitation began to constrict his body once again. Having his heart won over by something so uncertain was a bad omen. He told himself that he ought to have clearly seen the physical clarity of his punishment while in prison.

I am a changed person, I have repented, I have . . . His repentance was recognition of that clarity. Kōji's life had changed dramatically since the picnic at the waterfall. Lately, from the moment he got up in the morning, throughout the day, he waited for Yūko to bestow her smile on him. Moreover, when she did, he could only bring himself to think of this as evidence that she didn't love him after all.

Matsukichi jumped down into the sculling boat, hauled on the stern rope, and brought the craft in toward the stone steps of the harbor wall. Kiyoshi helped Kimi—who was carrying the ukulele—down into the boat. Kōji suddenly looked back in the direction of the ice plant. He watched as rays of golden light cascaded from the entrance—the door having been left open—spilling onto the dark concrete floor. It was a great outflow of silent, futile light—almost mystical in its appearance. He wondered why such a great amount of light jostled for space in that one place at night.

Taking up the oars, Matsukichi rowed the boat directly across the bay. Even out on the water, there was no wind.

Kiyoshi, who was a member of the Air Self-Defense Force ground crew, began to talk, enthusiastically, about dealing with the aftermath of a recent jet plane crash.

"There was an announcement on the speakers, giving the plane's current situation. It said, '*Emergency reported from: Flight Number T33A A/C number 390. The trouble is an engine stop. Present location above the Atsumi Peninsula.*' That was all. Then we lost radio contact. An F-86F fighter headed out right away to guide the plane down, but it radioed back that there was no sign of Flight 390. We were really shocked. Of course, two search-and-rescue helicopters had been scrambled as well. They carried out a fair number of low-level reconnaissance flights, and then, at last, we heard the sad news that they had found the crash site. We went separately by truck, and relying on guidance from the helicopters and using our own maps, we finally arrived at the scene about two and a half hours later. The body of the plane had plunged vertically into the ground. The tail, which we could just see sticking out of the earth, was smoldering and sputtering, and there was an indescribably unpleasant smell coming from the wreckage. I'll never forget seeing two helmets lying in a field, casting long shadows as they caught the westerly sun.

"It had already started to get dark, so the excavation and recovery of the bodies had to wait until the next morning. Besides, we hadn't even prepared any lighting equipment. We gathered together the fragments of wing that had scattered around the area, and then all we could do was pick some wild-flowers and spend the night offering them up with incense sticks in prayer. It was such a sad night. No one said very much. We threw up a rope barrier all around, thirty yards from the wreckage, and took turns to keep watch to make sure any onlookers couldn't get in. It was the saddest night I've ever spent, I can tell you. You have to appreciate, we're ground crew—used to carrying wrenches and screwdrivers, not guns. We weren't accustomed to standing guard like that. But, anyway, the long night passed without incident, and although the horrible stench from the burnt-out plane gradually faded, it clung to our noses all night long.

"Then morning came. The eastern skies brightened faintly. I remember thinking it would be an unearthly morning. I knew a gigantic round sun would climb into the sky. I wouldn't be able to bear to look at such a sun. Such an unbridled, dazzling sun. But before it came fully up, the unburnt tail section of the plane began to reflect the radiant first light of morning. It was so awfully beautiful. Then, for the first time, we saw clearly the horror of the accident."

"So, then what did you do?" asked Kimi.

"We started digging as quickly as we could. That was all," answered Kiyoshi, falling silent. Then he abruptly changed the topic of conversation and said, "We keep a small flower garden. When I say 'we,' it was actually the guys from the repair platoon who made it, although I help tend it now and again. We call it the 'Garden for the Attainment of Perfection.' It comes from the proverb 'Adversity is the best school.' It has a small rose-trellised entrance and a summer house we made from targets for shooting practice. There's even a red torii shrine gate on top of a miniature artificial hill, and goldfish swimming in a small pond, too. And scattered about in between are lots of flowers. There are carnations, and a cactus we planted recently was donated by the candy store at the PX. We also have some nasturtiums."

"Are the flowers dedicated to those who died?" asked Kimi.

"Don't be daft. Those flowers are there for the people who are still alive. But, tell me, if you're from Hamamatsu, too, how is it we haven't managed to bump into each other before now?"

"Because you haven't been at the base in north Hamamatsu for very long, have you? Besides which, there's no way you could find me in such a big town. Especially as I'm so good at hiding."

"See? That's how she is!" said Matsukichi, poking fun at Kimi as he slowly rowed the boat.

Kōji envied Kiyoshi his simple lyrical spirit. It was a warm, plump spirit, that was plain for all to see—just like a sweet bun in a shop's glass display case. There had been a flower

garden like the one Kiyoshi spoke of at the prison, too. While
Kōji hadn't helped with the garden that the other inmates
tended with such care, he had loved it timidly, superstitiously,
and keenly, and with a slight sense of loathing.

He, too, had heart-wrung memories of the vulgar saffron-
colored nasturtiums. But unlike Kiyoshi, he would never relate
such recollections to others.

And as for Matsukichi? He was like a dull-witted young
animal.

Kōji suddenly blurted, "Kimi, before, you made a promise,
right? That you'd have to leave some proof of your feelings on
the ukulele."

"When you say *proof*?"

Kōji explained that she ought to carve *With Love, Kimi* on
the body of the ukulele. Kimi hesitated a little but in the
end agreed. Kōji borrowed Kiyoshi's knife and inscribed the
ukulele in small English lettering. White granules scattered
as the lettering was scored into the glossy, dark brown surface
of the sound board. Kimi said she felt as though a tattoo were
being etched onto her own arm. Then she reached out and
softly touched Kōji's arm—tensed as it supported the ukulele
firmly against the slight pitching of the boat, so as to avoid
spoiling the lettering he was engraving.

The forest of Urayasu was located on the tip of the promontory, in an area within the breakwater on the end of which
stood a lighthouse. The eastern fringe of the forest gave out
onto a quiet inlet of the bay, while the western part of the forest spread immediately beyond the breakwater and connected
with the rocky coast of the open sea. In the midst of the dense
forest was a Shinto shrine, dedicated to the worship of an

early Kamakura-period sacred mirror known as the Shōchiku Hijaku Kyō.

It was known among the many small inlets in the bay particularly for its tranquility and white, sandy beaches—and they went intent on enjoying an evening dip in the sea.

The water close to the shore was extremely shallow and the bottom of the boat dragged on the sand. Stretching the mooring rope as far as possible, they finally managed to tie it to a rotten tree on the bank.

The three men were amazed at how well prepared Kimi was. When without hesitation she stripped off her beachwear, she already had on a white swimsuit. With no other option, the men swam in their underpants.

A new moon appeared in the sky above the village. Kōji could see the dull lights of the Kusakado house in the hills to the north of the village. With an invigorating shudder, he felt the uneasy, quickening pace of his heartbeat as his inebriated body was suddenly immersed in the water, and he swam about in the middle of the narrow inlet.

"Hey, a shadow! Look at the shadow!" shouted Kimi, lifting her head from the surface of the water.

Her gleeful cry slapped the water's surface and rebounded, drowning out the distant echo of breaking waves as they pounded the rocky shore. Looking down, they saw their own strangely distorted shadows on the white, cone-shaped seabed, lit up by the lighthouse twelve nautical miles away as it cast its beam across the darkness every two seconds.

Having enjoyed their swim sufficiently, they climbed onto the shore and entered the Urayasu forest. Even in the depths of the forest, the light from the lighthouse shone like a flash of lightning and transformed the unsettling darkness.

Although it was summer, the forest paths, ankle-deep in

moist leaves, were barely evident. The striped mosquitoes were a real nuisance. The deeper they went into the forest, the more the boom of the offshore waves echoed terrifically around the tree trunks.

Naked, they walked in silence, swatting at the mosquitoes that swarmed all around them.

"Let's light a fire here. It'll keep the mosquitoes away, and we can dry ourselves off," suggested Matsukichi. Kimi had only brought her ukulele, and so Kiyoshi went back to the boat to fetch matches. They made a small bonfire out of dead branches, and sitting around it, they all felt peaceful.

Kimi played her ukulele and sang softly, the fire reflected on the body of the instrument. Still wet, her bare shoulders took on a pale hue in the light of the lighthouse as it penetrated the lower branches of the trees. They neither laughed nor joked; instead, they were content in the feeling of superiority that came from indulging themselves in a special kind of pleasure, the likes of which they knew was alien to city dwellers.

They gazed in silence at the flickering flames of the small bonfire—the bottoms of their eyes stinging a little as the salt water dried.

"Give me the ukulele," said Matsukichi suddenly, his voice deep and serious. Resolution, following lengthy indecision, was clearly evident in his tone.

Kimi held the ukulele in her arms and refused.

"I won't."

They fell silent again. But this time the silence no longer carried with it that sense of calm.

Before long, Matsukichi pressed the matter again, more persistently and maladroitly than before.

"Now look. As I see it, there's three of us men here, okay? You have to give the ukulele to one of us, right? So I think you should give it to me."

Matsukichi's naked body was by far the most powerfully built of the three. He was broad-shouldered, and his chest muscles bulged like a bank of summer clouds. His voice, too, like his body, was imposing, though it carried with it a heavy, melancholy quality.

It seemed that Kimi sensed her answer at this moment would result in a definite consequence. Lifting her keen eyes, she stared at Matsukichi fixedly, and then, after they had glared at each other for a while, finally she said, "I won't."

It was obvious, even in the dark, that Matsukichi's face had begun to flush with embarrassment. All of a sudden he reached out a sturdy arm. Thinking only that this powerful lunge was directed toward Kimi, Kōji involuntarily moved his body diagonally in order to shield her.

Kōji had no idea how Matsukichi judged situations or how he made his decisions. Be that as it may, it was certain that his thoughts were seeking to escape from a kind of bewilderment in deciding to act the way he did. Ordinarily, he probably wouldn't have hesitated in fighting the other two men and choosing to take Kimi forcibly. And yet, in the moment, rather than trusting in his carnal desires (and, after this experience, he would be unlikely to doubt those desires again), he had put his faith in a single concept, that is to say, the ukulele. He snatched the instrument roughly from Kimi's grasp, and since Kōji had in fact been protecting Kimi's person, the ukulele was, if anything, easily taken. For some reason, in that instant, Kōji stole a glance at Kiyoshi. This serious young man's face was faintly immersed in a lyrical veil of unease, and with his mouth slightly agape, he looked as though he was bound to the depths of a world he found difficult to shut out—a world of flowers and aircraft tails glinting in the morning sun, a world filled with tragically heroic death. And yet, the lively scene that was in full play before him didn't call for honor on his part at all.

Kimi stood up and seized violent hold of Matsukichi's arms. The ukulele pitched and sailed dangerously into the air above their heads. In the end, Matsukichi couldn't resist Kimi's efforts, and instead he had tossed the ukulele to Kiyoshi. As if waking from a dream, Kiyoshi's naked body moved nimbly. He took the ukulele in one hand and began to run. Kiyoshi's actions were completely natural; he found himself in a situation where his role had suddenly become necessary.

Letting out an unhappy shriek, this time Kimi gave chase after Kiyoshi. But Kiyoshi threw the ukulele back to Matsukichi, who was now free of her. Laughing so loudly that his voice echoed through the forest, Matsukichi tore away in the direction of the beach by the inlet, throwing the ukulele once again to Kiyoshi's waiting hands. Then, while Kiyoshi and Kimi fought for possession of the instrument, he swiftly untied the mooring rope, splashed across the water, kicking up spray as he went, and leapt into the boat. As Kiyoshi plunged into the shallows, holding the ukulele above the water, Matsukichi tossed Kimi and Kōji's clothes onto the beach; then he reached out and pulled Kiyoshi into the boat.

Kimi cursed loudly from the shore. But she appeared to have abandoned any thoughts of swimming after them. The sculling boat, carrying Kiyoshi, Matsukichi, and the ukulele, receded in a moment across the bay, leaving Matsukichi's laughter trailing behind across the water. Before long, as the boat reached the middle of the bay—Matsukichi having handed the oars to Kiyoshi—the discordant sound of Matsukichi's strumming

reached the ears of Kōji and Kimi, left behind on the shore at
Urayasu.

There followed a predictable sequence of events. Kimi returned
to the vicinity of the bonfire in the forest and told Kōji that the
reason she hadn't swum after the boat earlier was because she
wanted to be alone with him. She said she knew full well that
Kōji was in love with Yūko, but that just for this one night she
was prepared to make a sacrifice and act as a stand-in.

Kōji hardly talked about how he felt. Kimi's doleful words
appeared absurd to him—like a set firework that hadn't gone
off properly. At length, he said he would prefer it if she didn't
talk anymore.

The roar of the ocean waves; the dying flames of the bonfire;
the beam of light from the lighthouse lancing like lightning
through the gaps in the trees; a new moon climbing into the
sky; countless stars . . . Surrounded by all of this, Kōji was able
to put Yūko from his mind and enjoy not having to think of
her at all.

He fancied he hadn't experienced the various contrivances of
nature befriending him like this since his youth, but appreci-
ating it now, it was like some elaborate chicanery: the artifice
of a new moon, the pounding waves, and the low, melancholy
buzz of mosquitoes around Kimi's hair.

When he buried his face in her magnificent bosom, and felt
her flesh—like taut sheepskin—on the tip of his tongue, he
unwittingly compared his rapture with that gem of perfect
flesh that had been honed by the young inmates day in, day
out, in the prison. In contrast to that, this was nothing but a
poor imitation. And people call this very thing nature.

Kimi's body was briny like a salted fish.

After they finished, she gazed deeply into Kōji's eyes as if trying to figure out how much he had enjoyed it; this was one of the things he wanted to tell her to stop doing.

Even so, Kōji's needs were sated. It had been a long time since he had experienced his sexual desires receding and leaving behind the flesh, as the waves turn and recede, leaving behind a wet beach.

Trying hard not to let his eyes reveal his gratitude, he held Kimi fixedly in his gaze, before planting a light kiss the way a man does after sleeping with his lover. For the first time, he thought, *I'm all body; just a physical presence—like a dog.* He felt as though, for a short while at least, he had escaped from his preordained destiny.

With their clothes tied up above their heads, Kōji and Kimi jumped into the sea below the lighthouse, and swam across the bay at its narrowest point. The tide was coming in and so there was no danger of being swept out to sea.

They reached the other side swimming between the oil-smelling boats, dressed quickly, and, barefooted, went their separate ways home.

Several days later, when he came down into the village, Kōji soon heard rumors about the young men. Apparently Kiyoshi was inseparable from Kimi's ukulele, carrying it around wherever he went. Kiyoshi's good fortune had become the object of envy of the young men in the village. And yet, no matter how much he was pressed, Kiyoshi just smiled, without revealing anything at all.

That night, Matsukichi asked Kōji to step outside the bar at the Storm Petrel as he had a confidential matter to discuss. He claimed that the night after they had been to Urayasu, he and Kimi met secretly and, finally, she gave herself to him. There had been a secret pact between Kiyoshi and Matsukichi. Kiyoshi cared only about his reputation. Matsukichi, on the other hand, was more realistic.

In exchange for keeping the ukulele, Kiyoshi had promised Matsukichi that he wouldn't lay a hand on Kimi. When Matsukichi confided this secret pact to Kimi, she suddenly began to laugh and then surprisingly easily, not to say cheerfully, agreed to his proposal. Matsukichi thought this proof enough that Kimi had been in love with him right from the start. He repeatedly impressed upon Kōji the need to keep this grave secret. If anything, Kōji was surprised that Matsukichi hadn't the slightest inkling of his own relationship with Kimi.

Kōji remembered his *geta* and Kimi's sandals that they had left in the forest in Urayasu that night. They had been kicked off carelessly—surely no one would mistake them for footwear discarded at the scene of a suicide. He hoped they would be taken by the incoming tide and carried out to sea as the tide ebbed, and how, if they weren't, then they would probably rot, half-immersed in water like a scrapped vessel. In the course of time, they would be eaten into completely and transformed into a dwelling place for an infestation of sea lice. They would cease to be *geta* and sandals. Having once belonged to man, they would instead melt into the great multitude of unearthly, formless material phenomena that exist on earth.

Chapter 5

Yūko seldom read the newspapers. It was as if she made a point of not doing so. Ippei was unable to read, and yet every morning he would sit for an hour or more holding the newspaper wide-open while moving his head lightly up and down.

Afterward, the newspaper would be passed to Teijirō and Kōji, who were working. There were times when they would get to reading right away with their heads buried in the pages. At others they wouldn't bother with the morning paper at all, instead preferring to wait for the evening edition to arrive.

That morning, when Kōji came out of the greenhouse, having finished spraying the plants, he noticed Teijirō, sitting on a decorative rock in the shade of a mimosa—a place he had decided would afford him protection from the heat of the day, intently reading a newspaper. The morning sun was already strong and the chirring of cicadas suffused the air.

Kōji came out of the orchid house—where plants such as the Indian Aerides orchid and the African Angraecum orchid grew in temperatures of seventy degrees Fahrenheit or more. As he drew near to where Teijirō was sitting, Kōji used his white teeth—instead of his fingers—to crudely scrape off a small leaf fragment that had stuck to his perspiring arm. As he applied his teeth, he saw close up his own deeply tanned arm.

It was like an insect's protective camouflage—the same splendid bronze color as the skin of everyone else in this village. Without being conscious of it, Kōji had waited to become adequately suntanned before he felt comfortable enough to frequent places like the Storm Petrel. His skin was no longer the conspicuous pale color it had been when he returned from prison. That sacred whiteness had disappeared from his flesh, and the sun had clothed him entirely in a new, flesh-colored undershirt that allowed him to blend in with the keen-eyed villagers.

He tried tasting the "sleeves" of his "undershirt." They were salty—exactly the same flavor as Kimi's body. A bovine, drab saltiness, devoid completely of any compassion or shame.

While Teijirō's back—clad in an old running shirt—was suntanned and magnificently towering, as he busily read the newspaper, it seemed to have lost its usual strength, and it appeared hollow, like a black cavern. The sparse gray hairs on the nape of his neck formed points of strong white light. Kōji recalled Teijirō one time bending over, just as he was doing now, while he mended a shirt. Looking closely at the small tears in the material of life, Teijirō had worked assiduously at repairing the shirt so that he might hurriedly shut out the long, dark hours of solitude that came spouting up from out of those small holes.

Teijirō hadn't noticed Kōji as he approached him from

behind, and so Kōji ended up reading the title of the article Teijirō was so engrossed in.

The headline read: *Aged dry-goods dealer strangles daughter.*

Suddenly becoming aware of Kōji, Teijirō instantly transferred his attention to a different headline. Kōji had never seen Teijirō react with such swift sensitivity toward another person before.

"You gave me a start. Creeping up on me unexpectedly," said Teijirō.

Then, roughly slapping the newspaper with his hand (at which point, a number of rose-pink petals that had fallen from the mimosa fluttered mysteriously on top of the news sheets), he pointed to a relatively small article and said, "Look at that. Seems like the typhoons will be early this year. We should make a start putting up the windbreaks."

"Yeah. Maybe tomorrow . . . ," said Kōji, a little haughtily, thrusting his thumbs into the front pockets of his jeans. This unmindful condescension was a little like flexing his muscles, experimentally, before posing his spiteful, probing question.

"Kimi returns to Hamamatsu today, doesn't she? She'll be along soon to say good-bye, I guess."

"That's right. She'll at least stop by to say good-bye, I should think," agreed Teijirō, vaguely. While there was no visible change in his strong face, it was obvious to Kōji that a crucible of ambivalent emotions boiled, almost audibly, within Teijirō's inner self.

Kōji recalled a box in which he kept several beetles as a child. Although one couldn't see through the surface of the thick, sturdy box, what was happening inside, like a gentle wave rolling into the shore, was evident from the bizarre burnt smell leaking from within and from the noise of the black, sluggish beetles locked in combat, their legs scrabbling for a foothold and the clashing of their horns. It was just the same as that . . .

Kōji had been taken by the sudden urge to thrust the blade of his pocketknife into that box and open up a hole.

He took another pace forward and said, "Kimi has got quite a reputation in the village. In more ways than one . . . Did you know that?"

"I know," replied Teijirō.

Answering without the slightest annoyance, Teijirō's mild tone aroused Kōji's suspicions.

Teijirō's head, with its close-cropped, grizzled hair, could well endure even the most direct sunlight. Sitting in the soft shadow of the delicate leaves of the mimosa, he seemed all the more incongruous and appeared to betray the immunity to anguish that Kōji secretly fancied Teijirō possessed.

Even the deep lines on his sun-beaten face—which in the past hadn't exhibited the slightest hint of anguish—now told of Teijirō's suffering. Undoubtedly, because they had been in plain sight, they hadn't drawn attention until now as a sign of that anguish; much like a ship's waterline—overlooked merely as a decorative stripe until the vessel is in peril.

Teijirō glanced at Kōji, squatting on the ground nearby. Using a twig, Kōji described triangles and squares in the dry earth and then, watching the irritation of several soldier ants as they tried to negotiate the disrupted path, he casually squashed them with the tip of the twig.

A small patch of earth became damp with the fluid from the ants' bodies. As the ants stopped moving on the ground, cracked by the harsh sunlight, it seemed that the world was experiencing a transformation so subtle that the world itself failed to notice.

With one large, darkly tanned hand, Teijirō tapped Kōji

lightly on the shoulder. Kōji turned around and could see from the old man's face that he was trying to say something—the words leaking out of the corner of his mouth like ripe fruit dropping to the ground.

When he spoke, he did so rapidly and with an extremely humble smile:

"Do you know why Kimi hates me? A little while after her mother died, I raped her. And then she left the house and went to Hamamatsu."

Aghast, Kōji stared fixedly at the old man's face. He was ill-equipped to deal with this, and it was clearly unfair that he should have to hear this sudden confession. Then Teijirō moved his left hand slowly around to the back pocket of his shorts.

Besides the countless wrinkles and bulging veins, Teijirō's yellowish, dark brown hands were a mass of small, old scars picked up from rose thorns, sharp leaves, from dwarf bamboo and cacti and the like. Added to which, they were smeared in a coating of earth and fertilizer so that, buried beneath this layer, the scars gave off a luster all the more dull. His scar-covered hand took from his back pocket an object like a protective amulet, wrapped carefully in a single sheet of plain white calligraphy paper. He opened it under the sunlight as it filtered down through the trees. His practically keratinous fingers made an exaggeratedly dry noise as they touched the paper. From the middle of the wrapping, Teijirō took out a photograph, stuck to a sturdy mount, and showed it to Kōji.

In the sunlight, Kōji didn't immediately realize what it was a picture of. The white part of the photograph was dazzlingly reflective and filled the middle of the picture, like a bank of clouds. He held it up obliquely to avoid the reflection. It was a photograph of a boy in a student's uniform and a girl in a sailor uniform performing sexual intercourse. Neither was wearing anything below the waist. Kōji was startled to see that the face of the girl student, who was lying on her back, resembled Kimi's. However, on closer inspection, it clearly wasn't her—only the area around her eyebrows bore a resemblance.

Revealing a healthy row of teeth that belied his age, Teijirō moved his eyes over the photograph, with a timid, humble smile. But the manner in which he thrust his face forward seemed impudent and overbearing.

"What do you think?" said Teijirō. "It looks a bit like her, doesn't it? I came by it one time I went to Tokyo."

Later, when he met briefly with Kimi to say good-bye, Kōji felt very miserable at the thought of the unsolicited story Teijirō had confided in him earlier.

It was a truly headstrong confession. Kōji didn't know to what end Teijirō had confessed to him. Perhaps there was no purpose. The raw sense of anguish that had been pent up for so long within the old fisherman had, in all probability, degenerated—like rice wine slowly turning into vinegar—and changed into an unpleasant, derisive sneer. The crime had already been dispelled. Kōji was fearful of the obscurely turbid way Teijirō was trying to live the remainder of his life. Discord, malice, an inability to forgive, whatever the circumstances—all these feelings were confused and mixed up in Teijirō's own indulgent reminiscences, lust, and indolence. Moreover, Teijirō's life, just like his face, had been steadfast. Anyone exposed to his derisive sneer would have been transformed into mere vinegar. That was true of Kōji, and Yūko, too, and even Ippei.

Kimi came up to the house empty-handed to say her farewells—having left her luggage at the Seitōkan inn. She said there were only forty minutes until her boat departed, and so she was restless from the moment she arrived. Sweating profusely down her light green dress, she hurriedly drank water from the tap near the entrance to the greenhouse.

Yūko had been preparing the midday meal with the young maid. Try as she might, the maid, who lived out of the house, just couldn't get the hang of cooking with propane gas. Since coming to this region, Yūko suspected that each of the five successive maids had engaged in propagating spiteful go-slow tactics. The hostility was always carried on the southerly wind, blowing up faintly from the direction of the village. And yet, to her face, they would always greet her in a plain and laid-back manner.

Kimi came around to the kitchen entrance, which faced a stone wall overgrown with ferns, and said, abruptly, "Hello there, ma'am. That smells delicious, doesn't it?"

"Oh, Kimi, it's you. I heard you are going home today? Won't you join us for lunch?"

"It's all right—thanks. I won't make the boat if I do."

Guessing that her open-minded husband would prefer it that way, Yūko had arranged it so that she and Ippei took their meals together with Teijirō. However, before long, Teijirō excused himself from this privilege and so from then on husband and wife developed the custom of sitting alone together at the dining table. Since Kōji had arrived recently, Teijirō had become all the more keen to behave in a manner befitting his status, with the result that Kōji ended up taking his meals with Ippei and Yūko. While Kōji received only a modest salary, he was treated as a guest when it came to food. It would have been a sensitive issue had Kimi joined them for lunch, and it was just as well therefore that she had declined the offer.

From the start, Yūko's cooking wasn't to the taste of country folk. She used butter and milk in applying herself to the creation of mock French cuisine, and one would think that she took the utmost care in preparing meals, but she could also be very slapdash with her cooking. Ippei never once complained about it, though.

Kimi talked hurriedly while she loitered in the doorway to the kitchen, and Yūko, who was frying snow peas—which produced a noise like a shower of rain—said without turning around, "Why don't you go and say hello to my husband. He's in the living room."

"Yes, I will," replied Kimi, causing the floorboards to creak as she came bustling up into the kitchen. As she passed behind Yūko, she asked, "Where's Kōji?"

"Kōji?" said Yūko, this time looking plainly over her shoulder at Kimi. Directing her reply at the large, slightly sweaty, quivering breasts right in front of her eyes, she said, in a low, stuffy voice, "I've just sent him to the temple on an errand with some flowers. Didn't you meet him on the way up? In any case, he should be back in time for lunch."

Kōji, who had run back up the hill from the temple, bumped into Kimi by the white rose–festooned archway, just as she was being seen off by Yūko. He had no idea why Yūko had come this far to say good-bye to her. She had probably just been passing by chance. Kōji glanced quickly through the gate, but there was no sign of Teijirō anywhere.

Having run all the way back, Kōji was breathing hard. He looked from one woman to the other without saying anything.

In contrast to Kimi's too-radiant face, Yūko's somewhat fading beauty, which she found difficult to disguise, gave her a refreshingly elegant appearance.

Having heard Teijirō's unsolicited story just a little while earlier, it seemed to Kōji that the force that overflowed from Kimi's slight frame must come from the effort of driving back the dark, filthy water that she was immersed in—just like an infant that, hating its bath, splashes water all around.

He understood now the way Kimi had looked at him after they had slept together, as if she was gauging his appetite for pleasure. She was watching to see whether she had infected him with the germ-like secret of her father's crime. She must have attempted to share her humiliating memory with many men without letting them know the truth. Her inclination was to revel in the web of deceit she wove around her sexual partners. It was this same inclination that compelled her to take advantage of Kōji, and to persuade Matsukichi to love her without giving him the ukulele.

That night when, pale in the flashing light of the lighthouse, with her eyes closed, Kimi had allowed him to caress her body while listening to the boom of distant waves, she must have been quietly picturing—over and over again—the origin of her burning, rejuvenating humiliation and self-loathing.

"Thanks for everything," said Kimi, greeting him plainly. "I'm working in the factory again from tomorrow."

"The typhoons will be here soon. It makes sense to return home around now, I guess," said Kōji.

As his ragged breathing returned to normal, his whole body broke out in a sweat.

"Quickly now, have a bath. You're soaked through with

sweat. Lunch will be ready soon. I invited Kimi to join us, too, but she says she won't be in time for her boat," said Yūko.

For some reason, Kōji hesitated and declined to go straight-away to take his bath.

Perceiving this, Kimi quickly said good-bye and began to walk away. Kōji stole a glance at Yūko to see whether she had noticed this sensitive reaction to his considerate action.

But Yūko only looked on with a vacant expression.

"Good-bye," said Kimi.

Kimi's eye suddenly flickered, like a berry bursting; then she gave him a conspicuous wink and squeezed his fingertips firmly together. Standing at his side and gazing at him for a while, she swung his hand gently to and fro.

Yūko put her hand to her hair.

Kōji stared only at Yūko, his heart overflowing with magnanimity. This was the first time he had been able to gaze at her with such composure. With the same vacant expression, Yūko inclined her face slightly and then slowly slid her hand across her hair. It was an uncertain movement, as if she were feeling her way through the midst of a dark and complicated memory. Dancing nervously, Yūko's fingers looked as though they had regained their old delicate and languid nature. Her fingers drew out a hairpin (in that instant, it caught the sunlight and shone a deep violet), and in an extremely perfunctory manner, she pricked the back of Kimi's hand.

Kimi let out a shriek and jumped back, laughing loudly from a distance. Stooping forward, she licked around the puncture wound, like an animal, and then she ran down the slope. Even after she had disappeared from view beyond the azalea hedge on the corner, her laughter could be heard intermittently, and Kōji fancied that, at the end of the dry path on that gentle slope, Kimi's lolling tongue was still flickering like a small apricot-colored flame.

Kōji turned toward Yūko with a fawning expression. Even with the intention of appealing to her better nature, he did so in high spirits, in a calm and carefree manner.

Taking care to ensure that he wasn't seen to be laughing along with Kimi, his smile became increasingly apparent.

Yūko turned her back on him and began to walk toward the house.

"Hurry up and take a bath. I can't stand the stink of sweat."

Glancing at her from the side, he realized that her brow was knitted in a deeply chiseled frown. It seemed it was just his perspiration that was on her mind. Perhaps she hated it.

The Kusakado family home was unnecessarily large. Ippei and Yūko slept in the detached ten-mat annex on the ground floor. In the main building, besides the ten-mat living room and the eight-mat sitting room, there were several small rooms that were not occupied, Teijirō's room at the back of the house, as well as a spacious kitchen and bathroom.

On the second floor was a twelve-mat guest room that was seldom ever used, and next to that a six-mat room where Kōji stayed. At night, they slept separately in their various rooms.

That evening, the air was still and humid. Unable to sleep, Kōji lay naked facedown on his futon inside a mosquito net, flicking through a lowbrow magazine he had borrowed from the village library.

He had been starved of reading material in prison, and one would have thought that Kōji had a strong intellectual craving, yet since coming here he had lost the appetite to read serious literature. He preferred the thick, lavishly colorful magazines—the kind with their pages curling at the edges, like the petals of a sullied artificial flower—that were stuffed full of scandal, comic strips, action dramas, and period plays.

Reading one section after another, he tried his luck with "This Month's Star Sign"—squinting at the fine No. 7 type print by the dim light of a reading lamp until his eyes were sore—and painstakingly pawing over the readers' columns.

> *28-year-old bachelor looking for friendship with a lady. Please write enclosing a photo.*

> *I'm a 20-year-old female shop assistant. Please write if you can go to the movies with me on my monthly two days off. I'll buy the tickets.*

> *Any ladies out there without family—please write. Let's console one another.*

> *Looking for carrier pigeons nearby at a reasonable price. Also looking for a male friend. 22-year-old factory worker.*

Lonely hearts, from all over Japan, jostling for space crammed into several pages of four-column ads in the magazine; solitude masquerading as cheerfulness was laid bare in just a few words.

What a great amount of loneliness. Such a strong desire to be loved. Pairing the lonely hearts up, as if playing cards, Kōji's well-trained powers of imagination saw the inevitable consequence of such rash exchanges of correspondence.

The couple finally meet, having exchanged countless letters: they discover in one another's faces the same kind of loneliness,

the same kind of neediness . . . And yet, out of impatience
to complete the mental picture they have already created for
themselves, the illusion is superimposed on yet another person
in a never-ending cycle—the awkward embrace, the morning
after—in the shabby hotel, breakfast in the diner, the carrier
pigeons that are kept on the roof, the same magazine, placed
by the statue of Hotei, the god of fortune, in the alcove, the
same readers' columns, hopes revived again.

Even though it was the middle of the night, it was unbear-
ably hot. Kōji repeatedly wiped away the sweat that ran down
the back of his neck. The smell of the new mosquito net that
Yūko had bought especially for him pervaded the inside of
the netting.

There wasn't even a slight breeze, and the stiff, light green
creases hung indignant, as if the net had just been put up, and
wherever the faint light reached, the fresh vermilion of the
corner ties shone vibrantly.

It was as if this vaguely distorted mosquito net intimated
the form of the world in which Kōji lived.

He had to get some sleep. He turned the light off and,
naked, lay spread-eagled. It felt like the sheet was a shadowy
image of his own being—absorbing the sweat that seeped from
his body.

As he lay there with his eyes closed, an image came to him
of the photograph he had been shown that morning, depicting
the girl who looked very like Kimi having sex.

He restlessly moved his body about, feeling his senses sharp-
ening like a knife in the midst of the wearily hot darkness.
Although the light had been turned off, a moth clung to the
mosquito net and scattered its tiny melancholy scales. He saw

its agitated shadow through the darkness. The moth struggled
for a while, before flying away through the open window.

The hoot of an owl. The transient cry of the cicada woven
in with the night. In the stillness of the night, he could even
hear the distant sound of the waves.

Kōji was afraid of this thick, gravy-like rural night. The
graphic quality of everything that lay in slumber during the
day awakening all at once was so much more physical than
nights in the city, and the night itself was like a colossal,
intense piece of meat saturated with hot blood.

His keen hearing detected the sound of footsteps coming
softly up the stairs. His body tensed as he watched through
the darkness. Kōji's six-mat room had a large north-facing
window, while the south side gave out onto a wide veranda
with a handrail.

In order to draw a breeze through, the rain shutters had all
been left open, and from where he lay he could see the vast
southern night sky.

The shadowy silhouette that had climbed the stairs stopped
and stood still with its back to the starry sky. It was Yūko,
wearing a peach-blossom-pink negligee. His heart throbbed
violently. He brushed the mosquito net aside and started to
step out.

"No, don't come out. You mustn't come out," said Yūko, in
a slightly stern voice.

Kōji hesitated and then crouched on top of his bed. Yūko
sat sideways on top of the loose south-facing edge of the mosquito net. As a result, that side of the net stretched tightly and
the securing cords—already mercilessly strained—quivered
dangerously in the two corners of the room where they were
attached.

"Come over here. Stay inside, though," she whispered, her dark face pressed against the net.

The scent of her perfume mingled with the night and came to him as he crawled up to her on his knees. The taut netting traced ever so lightly the curves of Yūko's body.

Kōji touched his shoulder against her rounded form. She didn't try to pull back.

"You don't know why I'm here, do you? You look surprised to see me," she said, in a cheerful tone, without hesitation. "It's a petty woman thing, you see. I didn't like the way you looked at Kimi when she was leaving for home. I stuck my hairpin in her hand, right? I couldn't stand to look at your face after that. Try as I might, I couldn't sleep thinking about it. That's why I came. You were so sure I was jealous, weren't you?"

Kōji nodded, but he managed to resist the urge to smile the way he had done that afternoon when Kimi was leaving.

"But you would be mistaken. I'm not the sort of woman who would do something like that out of jealousy. I was simply admonishing a conceited and discourteous young lady. When I do that, I don't use words; I use my hairpin."

Yūko seemed to hesitate before continuing. But, as if she was afraid that hesitating for too long would place an unnecessary burden on her words, she added, very quickly, "Just like the way you used that wrench."

Recognizing her defiance, Kōji decided against allowing himself to be drawn into an argument. Were he to rise to the bait and fly into a rage, he knew full well, since the picnic at the waterfall, that a different part of him would also become aroused. Instead, he assumed a meek demeanor and said, "So, basically, you've come here to speak ill of me once again."

While they may have been separated by the mosquito net—

their heads were close enough for each to catch the other's hushed words—their breath drifted around like mist. Yūko's breath was extremely fragrant. It seemed as though she had deliberately sprayed perfume in her mouth before coming in.

When he considered the time she must have spent on this preparation, her life's loneliness became clear to him. The hollowness of her life became quickly apparent with each perfumed breath. Yūko being this close made him feel all the more calm.

"Anyway, I'm a different person now. I've turned over a new leaf, you see."

"So have I," replied Yūko, a little proudly.

"There's no need at all for you to mend your ways. There was no need in the past either. I assumed responsibility for that crime so that you didn't have to have any regrets."

As he had suspected, his declaration angered Yūko. Pulling her shoulder away from him, she narrowed her eyes in a look of displeasure, and each time her words broke off, she cursed under her gasping breath.

"*Assumed responsibility*, you say? What a perfectly respectable way to put it! I didn't ask you to do anything. But if that's what you want to believe, then go ahead. What a conceited, fine, and chivalrous notion. And something else—you're forever playing the hypocrite."

After this, her rage having abated, she made a surprising confession in a flat, quiet voice. The tone of this confession had a lasting effect on Kōji.

Yūko's jealousy was directed not at Kimi, who was of no importance. It was directed, she said, at Kōji's crime.

The anguish she felt at not having a crime to her name

like the one he committed had grown in intensity. Ever since the picnic that day at the waterfall, this thought had rooted itself blackly in her mind—she wanted to compete with Kōji's crime, to somehow be able to own a crime like his in order to at least stand beside him.

Kōji mocked her at hearing this, asking Yūko if she thought committing a crime would make her a suitable woman for him, and telling her that she could try until she was blue in the face but it would be impossible to compete with him on that score. He hoped that his mockery would change her mind, like someone using harsh words to keep a person from losing consciousness.

In the face of these arguments, Yūko was preoccupied only with her own troubles and failed to notice at all that she had overlooked Kōji's suffering. If anything, Kōji was pleased about this. In Yūko's eyes, Kōji had, until now, appeared as someone who had committed and then atoned for his crime, as someone who at heart could be relied upon as a man of substance, a much happier individual than she was, and this, notwithstanding that Kōji himself would have said he had stood idly by watching fearfully as his sense of the crime and the associated remorse diminished with the passing days. Not that he could begin to relate to anyone else this nebulous sense of fear and unease. He felt as one would at watching a rainbow fade and disappear or watching that sacred hourglass in the prison bathhouse degenerate as the steam moves away, the backlighting is extinguished, and the cinnabar granules run out.

"It's hot, isn't it? I can't stand this heat," said Kōji.

"Yes, it's hot," said Yūko meekly.

The tops of her soft, swaying, slightly sweaty breasts were visible in the gloom through the light green material of the mosquito net. Only that part of her was immune to the dark and seemed to offer up its pale proof of purity. Yūko's lips were devoid of her characteristic heavy lipstick.

"Aren't there mosquitoes?"

"There aren't any. Maybe I'm not so tasty," she said, laughing for the first time and exposing her front teeth slightly.

Then, moving her face close to the netting, she stared intently—like she was examining the violently pulsating temple of this naked youth—as he squatted inside his quivering, light green cage.

Leaning over the mosquito net, she buried her nose in his shoulder and said, "You smell strange."

"It must offend you."

Without altering her position, she shook her head slightly.

This was the moment that Kōji had long been waiting for, and extending his arms, he tried to embrace her. Yūko's rancor disappeared, leaving only gentleness.

Kōji ought to have persevered a little more and slid out from the mosquito net or else adroitly guided Yūko inside. Instead, he took hold of her, mosquito net and all. The coarse cotton chafed roughly against his bare chest; one of the securing cords came away, and Kōji's body, too, was enveloped in a wave of cotton.

At that moment, he felt the smooth flesh inside Yūko's peach-blossom-pink negligee slip through his hands. Yūko, having already moved away from the broad veranda, was now standing near the handrail, pulling her displaced negligee back over her shoulder. Panting for breath, she stared at the quiet mosquito net, before transferring her attention to the garden below.

The glass roofs of the five greenhouses twinkled in the

moonlight. Signs of dark, squat vegetation could be seen at the bottom of the glass panes, which reflected the faint, bright outline of some evening clouds. They looked like deep, stagnant water tanks with large deposits of algae.

A white figure stood in front of the orchid house.

Sometimes, worried about the temperature regulation, Teijirō got up in the middle of the night. But that happened mainly in the winter. The white clothing was toweling pajamas—not the sort of thing that Teijirō wore.

Still looking toward the second floor, the figure began to walk toward them. The man was lame in his right leg.

"My husband's in the garden. He's coming this way. And he was sleeping so soundly, too!" screamed Yūko, no longer concerned about her loud voice as she turned to face the quiet of the mosquito net.

Kōji made no reply.

Seeing Ippei's approaching form gave Yūko strength. Drawing near the mosquito net, she gazed at Kōji as he lay sprawled on his back. He had his hands clasped behind his head and his eyes closed. She imagined how her sleeping form next to Kōji would have looked to Ippei's gaze. She felt that, if he appeared, in front of him she would be able to do anything.

The thought that even the things she hadn't been able to do without Ippei could be realized at this moment liberated her from a long-continued suffering.

From the moment he heard her scream, Kōji perceived a sudden, violent change in Yūko's heart—that was how well he had come to know her. And then, the sense of remorse, which had begun to fade, revived itself vividly and filled his heart with the docility of an ex-convict. It was a fondly remembered, tender emotion, and Kōji was attached to it.

"You mustn't. What you're thinking is wrong," he said, firmly pinning down the edge of the mosquito net with his body.

Yūko tried even harder to enter the net from a different angle.

This time, half-struck with fear, Kōji lowered his voice and said, imploringly, "Stop it, will you? I beg you. Stop doing that."

Her pride wounded, Yūko sat outside the mosquito net, with her back toward the north-facing window. She stared at him with an unmistakable look of hatred.

Kōji's eyes were dry and bloodshot, and in spite of himself, he stared hatefully at Yūko. He couldn't take his eyes off her.

Ippei's footsteps climbed the stairs. Strange footsteps, once heard, instantly recognizable.

Protecting his right arm and leg, his left hand clung to the handrail as he came ponderously up the stairs. It felt like he would never arrive. It seemed to Kōji like the stairs went on forever, ascending higher and higher.

Yūko stood up, and opened the sliding door to the guest room just a crack. Even during the summer, the door was properly closed in order to partition the two rooms; the partitioning wall was covered with things such as Kōji's desk and a small chest of drawers. Having not been opened for some time, the sliding door creaked and began to warp slightly in its frame, but she slipped adroitly through the gap and went into the twelve-mat guest room, closing the door behind her.

Kōji shut his eyes. He was lying with his head pointing north, and he was afraid of catching sight of Ippei over the edge of the mosquito net as he passed by the veranda.

"Yūko . . . Yūko," called Ippei, as he walked along the wide veranda.

"I'm in here." Her voice came trippingly from the dark, musty-smelling twelve-mat guest room.

With his eyes closed, Kōji followed only their conversation.

As the night wore on it started to get a little blustery outside. The wind, dissipated now as it sifted through the mesh of the net, played lightly on his skin, and all the more made him acutely aware of the oppressive heat.

"Cold," said Ippei. There was a needlessly assertive tone in his voice as he emphasized the word, almost like a stout, heavy stick tapping around in the darkness.

"Cold? It's not cold. You mean it's cool, don't you?" Yūko was saying.

"Cool . . . I want . . . to sleep here."

"Eh?"

"It's cool. Here. I want to sleep here . . . from tomorrow," said Ippei.

Before they set to work protecting the greenhouses against the approaching typhoon, Kōji and Teijirō spent the whole of the next day busily loading plants into the truck that had arrived, as it did at regular intervals, from Tokyo Horticulture. Tokyo Horticulture had a number of greenhouses around the Izu Peninsula with which it placed direct orders. The president had recommended that Yūko choose the area around Iro Village, since it was conveniently located to join the chain of their direct-order greenhouses that lay in range of the truck route.

In this way, in exchange for being paid by check each month, what was tantamount to a fixed commission by the head office, the greenhouse could do business without the fear of its prices being knocked down at market or the unfavorable competition from the foliage plants supplied direct from Osaka or the roses sold by Tokyo rose growers.

The three-ton truck from Tokyo Horticulture stopped by two or three times a month without fail, and then returned again loaded up with fifty or sixty potted plants each visit. Depending on the season, it would sometimes take as many as a hundred pots. In the summertime, it was mainly foliage plants and orchids. Unable to compete with the produce from areas around Den-en Chofu, the Kusakado greenhouse would ship the cheaper plants, such as gloxinia, to Numazu. These plants were removed from their pots and packed in boxes, and then Kōji took them by handcart to the port.

With great difficulty, the truck climbed sluggishly up the slope as far as the entrance to the Kusakado greenhouse. Yūko was concerned with looking after the drivers, giving them presents of things such as Ippei's Italian-made ties and English socks, together with a grandiose explanation of their origin.

When it was time for the shipment, Kōji always felt sad at parting with the plants he had cultivated with so much tender care. The cymbidium, with its leaves similar to those of pampas, displayed an elegance as though it had caught some kind of disease-like "beauty," through the form of its flowers, which float in the air like a sudden vision—a characteristic of orchids, together with its pale purple brushed petals, and lips with purple flecks scattered on a yellow background. To a greater or lesser extent European orchids had that same feel about them. The light red flowers of the dendrobium afforded a glimpse of dark purple in the depths of their tubes, yet they did not attempt to keep their bashfulness in the shade, rather, they seemed to explicitly reveal it. The Hawaiian anthurium was lurid red like synthetic resin with a rough feline tongue projecting from it. A seaweed-like delicate appearance of tiger

tail contrasting with the tough nature of its dark green spot-
ted leaves bordered with pale yellow. The large oval leaves of
the Decora, an improved variety of rubber plant. The Ananas,
with its audacious green bromeliad leaves sporting horizontal
black stripes. The lady palm with a profusion of glossy leaves
growing from thin hairy stems . . .

All these had left Kōji's care and were now lined up on the
dirty truck like a group of cold, silent prostitutes taken away
by the police. Kōji dreamed of the worlds infiltrated by his
dispersed flowers and leaves. He imagined a society of dazzling
immensity and grotesque pitch-dark complication where these
flowers and leaves hung, as if they were little ribbons secured
here and there over its body. The flowers were mere caricatures
there. These flowers and leaves would scatter and infiltrate
shrewdly, like germs, a variety of entirely useless places in
society for the purposes of practical sentimentalism, hypocrisy,
peace and order, vanity, death, disease . . .

After loading the truck, Kōji placed the wrapped gloxinia
on the handcart and hurried to the port to make the last shipment of the day. It was getting cloudier, and the wind had
started to rise.

He loaded the plants onto the boat and watched it as it
departed from the quayside. He noticed that the stern lines
of some fishing boats moored nearby were creaking more than
usual with a high-pitched whine. The quay where he stood
was bright in the sunlight. The sun was shining from the pale
blue sky in the west through a cleft in the thick clouds. Far
off, some shining clouds drifted tranquilly in the not-so-large
clear sky, as if it were a painting enclosed in a frame. The shape
of the clouds was like a gabion stuffed with copious amounts
of light . . . .

When Kōji got back, Teijirō was in a real fluster. He had

heard on the radio news that the typhoon was approaching much more quickly than expected.

Determined to work through the night, they set to the difficult task of sticking long, stout plywood sheets, which they had prepared specially, diagonally across the window frames of the greenhouses, and then further protecting the glass panes by hanging straw matting over the top.

After what had happened the previous night, Yūko avoided Kōji and obdurately did her best not to speak to him. Her attitude repeatedly hampered their busy work. But Kōji worked on diligently without complaint—a little like an unheeded child engrossed completely in the task in front of him. If anything, this state of rejection was necessary in order for him to find some value in his work.

Buffeted by the moisture-laden wind, which intensified as night came on, Kōji found the continuation of his earnest, silent labor agreeable. This work had been "bestowed" on him; it had been the same sort of labor that had delivered the prisoners from resignation to their oppressive fate.

The night wore on. Having progressed more quickly than he had expected, Kōji set about working on the roof of the last greenhouse to finalize their work. Climbing from the top of the ladder onto the roof, he straddled the ridge—taking care not to step on the glass panes—and took hold of the long plywood panels that Teijirō handed to him. To help them with their work, all the fluorescent lights were ablaze in the greenhouses, and the resultant brightness lent the garden an otherworldly appearance.

Thick clouds drifting in the sky jostled with one another. Kōji gazed down between his legs at the shapes of the flowers and plants inside the bright, still greenhouse—undisturbed by the wind outside. He fancied that he had never seen such self-sufficient flowers, quietly breathing in the night air, and unaware of human scrutiny. Furthermore, with their primary colors, this colony of statue-still flowers and leaves, crowded into the uninhabited interior of the greenhouse, created almost a sense of danger.

Cheerfully maintaining his balance in the face of the rain-laden wind—like a sailor perched on top of a ship's mast—Kōji hammered in one nail after another with a well-practiced hand, before shifting his body slightly and quickly driving a nail into the next sheet. The sound of the hammer rang clear as it pierced the warm wind. Just as he thought it would strike his face, the light rain receded and was now falling onto the top of the mimosa tree. He could feel the solemn, turbulent sky pressing down overhead. The wind gave Kōji's mind a colossal freedom of emotion, as if in an instant it would carry away into the boundless distance all his words. Mimicking a professional carpenter, he placed several nails between his lips. The indescribably sweet taste of the steel. He felt frighteningly free.

He saw Yūko—who was wearing slacks—come down into the garden from the edge of the veranda of the main building. When he recognized this ill-tempered mistress, his sense of freedom withered in a moment. It was well past her and Ippei's usual bedtime. She had what looked like a Coca-Cola bottle in each hand. It seemed she had come out to reward them for their hard work. As before, she decided not to speak to Kōji, but as she called out to Teijirō, her loud voice was broken and carried by the wind so that Kōji was able to hear only snatches.

"You've worked hard. Why don't you take a short break? Is there anything I can do to help?"

As she spoke, the scarf, which she had thrown on carelessly, was whipped away from her hair by a sudden gust of wind and blown high in the air, coming to rest on a corner of the glass

roof in front of Kōji. As the scarf came away from her head,
Yūko looked to Kōji like a beautiful animal, with her flame-
like, tangled mass of hair. Holding the bottles in her hands,
she had been unable to save her scarf from the wind. Placing
the bottles by the entrance to the greenhouse, she raised her
hands in the air. One half of her face appeared pale in the light
of the greenhouse, and her unsmiling countenance lifted and
for the first time turned toward Kōji—as if in prayer.

Kōji reached out and took hold of the scarf. A design of ivy
had been hand-painted in gold on the extremely fine black
georgette. At once, he spat the nails out and wrapped them in
the material to hold the scarf down, and then shouted, "I'm
going to throw it. There's a weight inside, so keep out of the
way."

Yūko observed Kōji's movements closely and gave an affir-
mative nod. With a feeling of mild admiration, she watched
as Kōji's youthful form adopted a throwing position against
the agitated gray night sky, sitting astride the greenhouse roof
with the wind tugging at his clothes. The scarf balled into a
small black mass and dropped to the concrete floor in front of
the greenhouse.

She drew near and, cautiously reaching out—as if it were an
unfamiliar object—touched her hand against the scarf. Then
she shook out the nails, stroked her hair, and, this time just
to make sure, tied the scarf ends securely under her pale chin.
Then she stood up and waved at Kōji on the roof. She smiled
at him for the first time since the previous evening. Without
applying too much or too little pressure, Kōji used his jeans-
clad thighs to brace himself against the sloping glass and his
body appeared all the more as if bound to the roof. Yūko's
actions seemed to him a selfish sign of reconciliation.

In the end, the typhoon veered away from West Izu.

Kōji had a patient debate with Teijirō about whether they ought to completely remove the protective sheets they had gone to great lengths to fix in place. Ultimately, they decided to leave half of them in place so that the sunlight would not be impeded. There was no way of knowing when the typhoon might come again.

One afternoon, several days later, Kōji was delivering some flowers to Taisenji temple. Yūko had asked him to take them that morning. He wasn't sure why, but he wanted to meet with the priest, who, whenever Kōji came, would always persuade him to stay awhile and serve him tea. Then he would invite him to sit on a cushion at the edge of the veranda overlooking the back garden, where, as always, the honeybees droned. The priest, Kakujin, didn't seem the slightest bit interested in probing into Kōji's affairs, and yet, in looking at Kōji's face he appeared to have detected something from his irritation-fueled put-on cheerfulness and from his red eyes—the unmistakable consequence of too little sleep.

Of course, Kōji didn't say anything either. He had not come to talk.

The night of the high winds, when he returned to his own room after that moment of reconciliation with Yūko, Kōji had sensed something was different. Without any prior notification, he discovered that the twelve-mat room next to his had been turned into Yūko and Ippei's bedroom.

As a result of his intense fatigue, Kōji had slept soundly that night. But the following night he couldn't get to sleep. *I'll get used to it before long*, he thought. After all, he had even become accustomed to that dirty bathhouse and the three-minute-interval buzzer.

In any event, it would likely take him a long time to grow used to it, and when he finally did, it was clear that something had definitely come to an end. Kōji was reluctant to suggest to Yūko that his room be moved downstairs, next to Teijirō's room or someplace like that. The reason was that Yūko hadn't notified him at all of her own room change (and clearly she was doing as Ippei desired!); added to which, Kōji's self-respect implored him to protect his small six-mat castle.

Incidentally, this slight rearrangement in the pattern of living in the Kusakado household had, by the following day, suddenly become general knowledge throughout the village. The young maid who lived out of the house had made sure everybody knew about it.

The villagers delighted in the fact that this strange family had at length come to this pass. There was pleasure in guessing how their immoral behavior would turn out. Several mothers with disabled children expected that before long a child more conspicuously ugly and deformed than any in the village would be born to the Kusakado household.

A child that would play tag with its own shadow, weaving in and out of the dozens of oil drums lined up at the harbor, the sides of which were brightly colored in the sunset, who, teased by the young, fit fishermen, with his tongue dripping saliva, would try to help load the cargo onto the ship. Doubtless, such a child would grow up to be like those mothers' own sons . . .

The rumors were reported that day to the priest's wife, as a consequence of which the priest, too, soon got to hear of them. The priest had just returned from holding a Buddhist service for the dead. When he heard about them, he fell silent, took hold of the sleeves of his black vestment, and spread his arms out wide. He recalled a line from "Yun Men Stretching Out His Arms" in the *Hekiganroku*.

The priest's affection for Kōji positively overflowed from his affable, small, narrow eyes. It seemed clear to Kōji that he was weighing in his own mind what he was able to impart. Dimpling his ruddy cheeks, and in an extremely circumspect manner, the priest hesitantly began to talk. This was an indication that he was trying to step outside his own small-framed portrait.

"If there is anything I can do, then I will do my best to help. I would even take counsel with you. You seem to have much that is weighing heavily on your mind. If you are worried about something, it is better to get it off your chest. The soul, you see, is a shy and retiring thing. It lurks in dark places and dislikes sunlight. And so, if you do not keep the skylight open at all times, the soul will rot. It easily decays, like a fresh sea urchin."

While he appreciated the priest's concern, this sort of excessive decorum about the heart and soul only served to arouse Kōji's suspicions. The priest talked about the soul hesitantly, in a tone that almost suggested he was discussing Kōji's crime. In that instant, Kōji fancied he saw through the priest's clumsy way of interrogation. It was like an inexperienced fisherman trying to extract a lobster from inside a creel.

Had he been a little more experienced in his handling of such situations, the priest ought to have approached Kōji seemingly oblivious to the existence of the soul within and, before Kōji himself had realized what he was doing, skillfully and in no time at all plucked it out by the short hairs. And, if he had succeeded in this, then Kōji, whether willing or not, would no doubt have confided everything.

This bald-headed priest, with his shiny, ruddy complexion and clean-shaven round face . . . Discussing and asking questions about his soul in that halting manner only succeeded in causing Kōji to shrink back.

Why are you talking about my soul? Can't you deceive a young guy like me more skillfully? Shouldn't you be appealing to my manhood, rather than my soul?

Kōji remained silent, and so the priest spoke again. "Yūko-san . . . she is a fine woman—"

"Yes, she's a fine woman, all right," interrupted Kōji quickly. "I owe her a lot. But, sir, you must be the only person in the village who says nice things about her."

"Well, that's all right, isn't it? I will vouch for her."

"In that case, we'll all go to heaven then?"

With this rejection, Kōji brought the conversation to an end, and the silence was filled with the drone of the honey-bees. If anything, Kōji had been hoping for a strong rebuke from the priest, but that was probably asking for too much. While he had stepped up to the threshold of this young man's soul, in the end the priest withdrew timidly. Kōji detected in this something akin to the restrained respect society showed toward an ex-convict.

This young man had acquired the privilege of misunderstanding people's reserve. For him, adopting an ostentatious, gentle attitude appeared to be the real reserve, the only genuine modesty.

In that lightning-like instant, Kōji felt disappointed by the priest. He had failed to comprehend at all the hurricane-like speed with which Kōji had fallen into a state of despair.

So the priest stepped back from Kōji at that moment and pinned his hopes on the near future; someday this young man would open his heart and meekly seek the priest's instructions.

Then surely he would be able to attain the heights that no one else his age was capable of.

Although a harsh westerly sun shone down on the back garden, it disappeared behind the many clouds that scudded across the sky, repeatedly throwing the garden into shadow.

At that moment, Kōji noticed Ippei and Yūko coming slowly down the slope opposite the garden. It was evidently time for Ippei's walk. Kōji was suddenly seized with the urge to hide from them. If he were to escape into the inner temple and hide in the shadow of one of the pillars draped with fraying gold-threaded banners or perhaps conceal himself in the shadow of the Buddhist image dais, which was enclosed by a railing with its inverted lotus-carved posts—and where it was dark even in the daytime—they would not pursue him that far. He would hide there forever. How nice that would be, he thought.

However, the couple stopped abruptly just at the point where they could look down on the priest's living quarters. With no alternative, Kōji came down from the edge of the veranda and stood in the garden. But the couple hadn't stopped because they had seen him; rather, they had bumped into the wife of the postmaster, who was just then on her way up to the Kusakado greenhouse. The postmaster's wife was a licensed flower-arrangement teacher who taught the young ladies of the village, and as such, she was a special customer of the greenhouse, buying her flowers direct.

Yūko started back up the hill in order to show the postmaster's wife some flowers. But then, noticing Kōji for the first time standing in the back garden of the temple, she called to him.

"Ah, that's perfect. Kōji, would you mind accompanying Ippei on his walk today?"

Strangely, although three months had passed since Kōji had
first come to these parts, this was the first opportunity he had
had of spending any real time alone with Ippei. In fact, it
occurred to him that this was the first time since the occasion
when Ippei, on a mere whim, had invited Kōji—then still a
student—to the bar for a drink.

Kōji couldn't help subconsciously comparing Ippei, as he
was in the bar that night, with the man who now walked
beside him. While this invalid seemed to be the sort who
would prefer going for a stroll after sundown, in fact he liked
to go out with the westerly sun at its strongest, wearing a straw
hat. Ippei was afraid of the vast darkness of the countryside at
night.

The walk took an exceedingly long time, owing largely to
the frequent, lengthy stops that Ippei made in order to rest.

They turned their backs on Yūko and the postmaster's wife
and began to descend the slope. Ippei was placed in Kōji's care,
and an incessant, mellow smile appeared on his face. Amid the
dazzling glare of midday, Kōji found it impossible to imagine
his sleepless nights. He wondered why, thanks to this invalid
with the helpless smile, the nights weighed heavily on him.
Why, when the days allowed him so much freedom, did the
nights turn so against him? During the nights he couldn't
sleep, Kōji discovered his hearing was sensitive to even the
slightest sound, and each time he heard Ippei's faint snoring
or an occasional sigh from Yūko—who also found it difficult
to sleep—escape over the top of the sliding door, he felt as
though his body was on fire. The twelve-mat room next to his
was like one of the greenhouses in the dead of night. Beneath
the light of the stars that shone down through the glass roof,

the plants continued their subtle chemical action—with little or no movement they dropped leaves, lost petals, and released persistent smells, and some gradually decayed where they stood. The exaggerated rippling noise as Yūko tossed around in her hemp futon. The faint sighs like the flickering of fire-flies. The billowing mosquito net . . . Finally, Yūko had once called Kōji's name. He had thought his ears were deceiving him, but when he quietly called out Yūko's name in reply, her voice came to him again, as if searching and hoping for the light of a distant village through the darkness. Just then, Ippei, who had been having a nightmare, cried out in his sleep like an animal and looked as though he would come to, only to settle down again . . .

They came down to the level ground. The surface of an unhar-vested paddy field and a cornfield stirred in the wind. As it swept across the green rice paddy, the pliant leaves revealed their white undersides, and each time a cloud passed over, the field appeared desolate. Then the sun would begin to shine again. A white line of parched road stood out in dazzling relief.

Kōji began to think that speaking slowly and clearly in order to make himself understood for Ippei's benefit was pointless.

Rather than telling him what he thought, the effort required to make Ippei understand through this narrow interaction made a mess of his attempted communication.

There was so much Kōji wanted to say, so much he wanted Ippei to understand, and so much he himself wanted to know. He felt he ought to say candidly exactly what he thought and, suddenly, stepping over the line he had been hesitant to cross, he summoned the courage to speak to Ippei audaciously.

"Say, I just can't understand the way you behave. Why do

you spend your time tormenting Yūko and me with that sim-
pering grin? I've been wondering but . . . You hate me, don't
you? Well? Isn't that right? Why not come out with it and say
it like a man? When things are going conveniently for you, you
make out that's exactly how you intended it, but when things
are not going too well, you blame it on your illness and then
just deliberately leave things vague and unresolved. Isn't that
true? Hey!"

Kōji prodded Ippei lightly on the shoulder as he walked
beside him. Reeling, Ippei eventually steadied himself by
leaning on his walking stick; he shook his head slightly and
uncertainly, and that stubborn smile spread across his face.

Just talking rapidly this way lifted Kōji's mood, in addi-
tion to which, strangely, he even felt a sort of rough friendship
toward his helpless companion.

"You say it's not true?" he said, continuing. "Good heavens!
You understand everything I say, don't you? What a despicable
guy you are. I've never met anyone as loathsome as you."

Ippei shook his head helplessly once again. His rough
friendship rejected, Kōji felt deflated. Moreover, he felt that
when it came down to it, what he really wanted to say was
exceedingly simple and didn't require a great many words.
Everything there was to say had been said without saying a
thing, and once it was put into words, it all fell apart so easily. And yet, he dared to continue his rant. Kōji reckoned this
would be his only chance to talk to this ash-like man, as one
human being to another.

"The truth is, you resent me. You're angry with me, aren't
you? You don't even want to look me in the face, and each
time you do, all you think is that you can never forgive me.
But, when Yūko invited me here, I wanted to see your face.
Even though I was afraid of what I might find, for some reason

I wanted to see it. I hoped that if I lived my life side by side
with you, then I might be able to become a decent person. Do
you understand? It's like making a child regret breaking a toy
by forcing him to live with it. You can't just buy him a new
one. So long as I'm with you, I had the feeling I could mend
my broken life. Do you see what I'm saying?"

Still maintaining his smile, Ippei moved his eyes restlessly,
as if from the fear of being suddenly confronted by something
that was difficult to understand.

*This man's soul is beginning to struggle behind a wall that has no
exit*, thought Kōji. *Although he is not cognizant of the goings-on
in the world, he can hear sounds outside—he can hear the knock at
his door.*

Now, Ippei didn't complain he was tired. If anything, he
gave the impression he was trying to get away from Kōji—
animatedly thrusting his walking stick and left leg forward and
forcing his unwilling right leg to follow as he continued doggedly in his characteristic mechanical gait—striking out along
the wide, dusty road that ran past the post office toward the
village shrine. On the other side of a small arched stone bridge,
surrounded by gigantic camphor trees and ancient cedars, the
main building of the shrine stood quietly at the top of just six
stone steps. The precincts of the shrine were extremely small,
and the calm of the place was disturbed by the noise of min-
ing, coming from a neighboring quarry over to the left. The
area produced high-quality pyroxene andesite, which K Stone
Merchants dug out and shipped mainly to Chiba Prefecture.
Even during the heat of the summer, the noise from the compressor sounded continually, causing a delicate vibration in the
air—like the wingbeat of an insect. Having finally walked this
far without a break, Ippei sat down on the low stone handrail
of the arched bridge, close by the shrine. Shielded by the deep

shadows from the trees, from where both the shrine precincts
and the quarry could be seen, Ippei liked to watch the stone
tumble down as it was hewn from the rock face.

"It's hot," said Ippei.

"Yes, it is," agreed Kōji, applying his handkerchief—which
was already dirty from wiping away his own perspiration—to
the beads of sweat forming on Ippei's brow. Compared with
the words that Kōji had earnestly spoken up to now, only these
words had about them a human quality. Ippei reduced his
intercourse with the human world down to this one point,
and rejecting everything else, it appeared as if he was trying to
control those around him from this narrow perspective.

"I bet you like to dress up like this for the girls in Ginza,
don't you?" continued Kōji, venomously. "I bet they laugh
their socks off when they see those baggy khaki trousers, and
those slip-ons, not to mention that uncouth open-collared shirt
and that straw hat. And the way you sometimes slobber. Who
on earth are you trying to impress in this fancy-dress costume?
If you asked Yūko, she'd say you wear this getup because you
like it, but what hasn't changed is your resolutely bad fashion
sense. You're playing out the crime. You've assumed the shape
of it. And I know you've done that to make a point to Yūko
and me. I'm going to peel off the layers of your disguise. It's
certainly not my fault you are the way you are. That's what
you want, isn't it?"

"Wa . . . nt?" said Ippei, dubiously, still smiling.

But Kōji was no longer prepared to listen.

"That's right. You do this of your own free will. I've gradually come to realize it. You intimidate us using false pretenses;
then you try to convince us that those false pretenses are indis-
pensable. You're making a real good job of it. Without you,
Yūko and I wouldn't have come together. And yet, so long as

you are here, Yūko and I can never be together. This strange relationship has come about because of your machinations. We can't even kiss each other without thinking of that incident; memories of the crime taint its taste and turn it to ash. You're conducting yourself just beautifully. You are waiting to see everyone prostrate themselves before you. It's what you've wanted all along. Well, isn't it?"

Kōji realized that Ippei wasn't listening to a thing he said and instead was bent over the stone handrail, staring fixedly at a long-horned beetle that had stopped there for a moment, and because he was motionless—hesitating as if he was about to place his straw hat over it, and the long-horned beetle, too, was stock-still on the surface of the cool stone in the shade of the trees—Ippei looked as though he were waiting for the assistance of some outside force to suddenly shorten the fixed distance between himself and the beetle.

Kōji seized him by the scruff of the neck and gave him a yank. Ippei lost his balance. With his backside barely remaining on the stone handrail, his withered arms and legs seemed to float in the air, and with his head inclined, he watched Kōji's face intently.

"Hey, pay attention to what I'm saying. Don't look so serious. Try smiling the way you always do."

Kōji lightly brushed his left index finger against Ippei's lower lip. Ippei's mouth immediately slackened, and as if mirroring Kōji's own laughing mouth, it took on the shape of his customary smile.

"All right. Now listen to me carefully," continued Kōji, moving his hand away. "You are content with things the way they are. You even think that it would be your salvation if everyone followed your example and did as you do. You, at any rate, are alive. However crippled you may be, you're alive, and that's something. You're taking a splendid vacation that has turned up at the end of the things you used to do: the flamboyant life you led when you were young; the artistic literary works you wrote, pouring scorn on others; and your uncontrollable preoccupation with the opposite sex. It's just one long vacation. You're forever making a show of that empty, splendid vacation, and now you are able to show off openly all of those thoughts you have harbored for so long. *I don't care much for people . . . Ah . . . ah.* And then you slobber. You just grunt in response to the notions that people hold dear and turn them into something meaningless. *Will? . . . Ah . . . ah . . .* You turned the desolation of your soul into your prerogative, and you order others to respect that right. Eh? Yes, everyone makes choices and continues to behave as they wish. So, what's so bad about me? What is it you hate about me? Come on, out with it! Say it! Say it, won't you! Was it wrong of me to pick up that wrench from the hospital garden? You put it there, having discovered that was where Yūko and I were to secretly meet, didn't you? Well? Admit it! Tell me what it is I have done wrong!"

Just then, the half-naked quarry workers hurriedly divided into two groups and dodged a large rock fall. The stones kicked up a cloud of dust as they rolled down the cliff—revealing a fresh section of rock that glittered in the sunlight—and reached as far as a clump of tall-stemmed summer grasses before subsiding inelegantly.

The muscular, sweat-soaked backs of the workers were lightly covered in white dust from the stones.

Having witnessed the rock fall, an almost indescribable expression of delight surfaced on Ippei's face. His eyes brimmed with ecstasy, while his nose seemed to detect the invigorating stench of death; a faint flush came to his suntanned cheeks. In that instant, Ippei's trademark smile, which revealed his white teeth, appeared quite beautiful to Kōji.

As if to spur himself on, Kōji continued to speak. Ippei's silence, while Kōji was quiet, disoriented him, and he fancied that Ippei, not grasping at all what he was saying, had afforded him a glimpse of the uncanny abyss within him.

"To tell the truth, thanks to me taking that wrench to your head, your thoughts are now complete; you've found a pretext for existing. What does life mean? Life for you is the inability to speak. What is the world to you? The world is your inability to speak. What is history? History is your inability to speak. What about the arts? Love? Politics? Everything and anything is your inability to speak, and so everything is coherent. The things you have been thinking about all along have come to fruition. But that was in the days when I imagined that all that was left intact within you was your intellect, and that, like a clock that has lost its dial, only the mechanism moved with vigor, 'tick tock'—ticking away time with clockwork precision. But now I realize there is nothing inside you at all. I know it, because I have sniffed it out—like the people of a country who have long been unable to mourn their lost king, his death having been kept a closely guarded secret.

"Our household has begun to revolve around the hollow cavern that lies inside you. If you try to imagine a house that has a deep and empty well with its mouth agape right in the middle of the parlor, that would be about right. An empty hole. A hole so large it would swallow up the world. You safeguard that dearly, and not only that, but you arranged Yūko and me around the periphery in a manner that suits you and took it into your head to create for yourself an entirely new family of the kind that wouldn't have occurred to anyone else. An ideal, splendid family centered on that empty well.

"When you moved your bedroom next to mine, you were at last close to achieving your objective. Before long, three empty holes or wells had been completed, and you intended to create an intimate, happy family that was the envy of others. Even I felt seduced by it. I almost wanted to lend a hand and make it happen. If I'd wanted to do it, it would have been easy. We could have discarded our troubles, dug ourselves a hole as big as yours, and, right in front of your very eyes, Yūko and I could have had done with it and slept together like a pair of frolicking beasts without a care in the world. We could have writhed around in front of you moaning with pleasure and then, finally, fallen asleep snoring. But I couldn't bring myself to do that. And neither could Yūko. Do you understand? We simply couldn't do it—afraid as we were of turning into sated beasts and seeing your plan succeed. And what makes it all the more unpleasant is the fact that you are aware of this.

"I've gradually come to realize this since the picnic at the waterfall. When I was talking to you just now, I suddenly felt sure of it. Yūko fell victim to your machinations, and while she came dangerously close to helping you realize your plan, after everything even she couldn't bring herself to do it. You knew that.

"What on earth are you hoping for? While realizing we can't do it, you still seek to entice us. You corner us, knowing that we have nowhere to go. A common spider is better than you. At least a spider spins its own web and tries to ensnare its prey. You, on the other hand, don't even spin out your empty existence. You don't expend any effort at all. The vacuous being that you are wants to be at the sacred center of your empty world.

"What did you expect? Tell me! What do you want?"

Kōji's line of questioning became increasingly fervent as he found it more and more difficult to tolerate this monologue that Ippei would never comprehend. He once again fell victim to his own irritation in trying to make Ippei understand his questions, as before, and when this happened, his eager voice faltered and took on a mean-sounding tone again.

"What is it you want? Well? What do you really want to do?"

Ippei had been silent for a long while.

Just then, the western sky above the harbor started to glow with the setting sun, and the pebbles on the road cast their long shadows across its surface; as they did so, the first tears Kōji had seen Ippei shed spread thinly over his eyes.

"Home . . . I want to go . . . back home."

Kōji felt betrayed by this childlike supplication and was seized with anger.

"That's a lie. Tell me the truth. I won't let you go back until you do."

Once again Ippei fell into a long silence. Then, still sitting diagonally across the stone handrail, he gazed fixedly at the radiant western sky. Normally uncommonly dark and agitated as he tried to express many differing emotions, his eyes—more animated than in the past but not as vivid as those of a healthy person—were now completely still as they regarded the sunset, his irises openly reflecting the radiant western skies. The tightly congealed clouds were edged with yellow and crimson as a yolk-colored blaze of light streamed across the heavens.

Due to the sun, which had yet to go fully down, the promontory on the opposite side of the inlet appeared unnaturally bright green; the distance across the bay became impossible to gauge, and black protrusions—the ships' masts and the ice-crushing tower, which were only slightly more prominent than the rows of houses on this side—appeared to directly touch the promontory. The crimson reflection extended unexpectedly far into the distance, like sprinkled droplets of ink, and a section of the clouds directly overhead was also faintly tinged with red. The light from this magnificent sunset, which was at once intense and at the same time strangely calm, converged precisely in Ippei's unmoving pupils, and that minute melancholy image was not only projected into his eyes but also passed through his pupils and seemed to occupy every recess of his hollow interior.

Thrusting his walking stick into his right hand, he described something like characters in the air with the index finger of his unencumbered left. But the strokes were unduly confused, and try as he might, Kōji was unable to follow the invisible letters being traced in front of him.

"Why don't you try saying it," said Kōji, this time with the deliberate consideration of a doctor speaking to his patient.

With a dry, rasping voice that passed through his teeth, and with great concentration, Ippei spoke, expressing himself two ways—as he always did when he was afraid of being misunderstood:

"Death. I want to die."

As they followed the way home, they saw Yūko coming toward them on the path that went between the green rice paddies. Concerned that they were taking so long to return, she had sent the postmaster's wife on ahead and come back to meet them. With Yūko's back to the sun, which had almost gone down, her shadow soon reached their feet as she slowly drew near. The closer she came, the more attractive her heavy lipstick was against her face—the paleness of which was accentuated by the dark blue material of her cotton robe.

"You're taking your time, aren't you?"

"We've been chatting about all sorts of things," said Kōji.

"Chatting, you say!"

With the evening sun just then cast obliquely across her face, Yūko suddenly pulled the corners of her mouth back so that even the fine creases on her thin lips were visible and her lipstick shone in the light, and spoke contemptuously, with a note of deliberate surprise in her voice.

"It's nice and cool in the evening. It sounds like there are a lot of cicadas out lately. Anyhow, since we're here, do you fancy walking a little farther, toward the harbor? Are you tired?"

Ippei understood Yūko's question without any real difficulty. His customary smile surfaced below the straw hat as it slowly bobbed from side to side.

"Well, then, let's take our time. Thanks for your help. It's my turn now."

She moved between them and, with Ippei on her right side and Kōji on her left, set off walking. Before long, the path that ran due west cut across the prefectural highway and went straight to the harbor.

"*To the family members of the crew of the* Tatsumi Maru, *please come now and collect your five days' supply of rice.*"

The sound of the fishing cooperative's loudspeaker echoed around the hillside; accustomed to such announcements, people usually heard but didn't listen to them. And yet, when one thought how both the end of the fishing season holiday and the departure of the fishing boats were near at hand, it sounded unusually new.

Matsukichi's boat had already set sail toward Hokkaido. A

yellow cloud rose in the distance on the prefectural highway, followed by a dull rumbling noise. Half-enveloped in the dust, the body of a passing bus was barely visible. The glowing sky gradually lost its color, and the sun having already vanished behind the promontory in the distance, the headland stared blackly back at them.

While guiding Ippei, from time to time Yūko's left hand came into contact with Kōji's right. Sometimes the contact was soft, and sometimes it was hard and painful. In the end, Yūko's fingers, groping in the dark, lightly squeezed and then let go of his hand.

Kōji glanced at Yūko's face, but her head was facing directly to the front, and in profile, her face had a hard edge to it, as if she were curbing her desires. For a moment, there was a tired convulsive strength in Yūko's fingers as she squeezed and then released her grip.

Kōji started to speak. "You know, I'm always thinking that maybe my life is being lived just for his sake."

"*His*? You mean Ippei, right?"

Seeking to evade the issue, Yūko returned the question, but of course Kōji was referring to Ippei.

"Yeah, that's right," he continued, in a heavy, faltering voice. He let his head droop, and gazed at their feet slowly extending alternately forward as they fell in line with Ippei's pace—like some kind of ceremonial procession—on top of the white path that was just starting to go dark. "A lot of things have happened. But, in the end, I feel like I've behaved and lived exactly the way he wanted me to. And that will probably carry on this way from now on as well."

Kōji did his best to sound nonchalant, but Yūko's intuitive power surprised him.

Her shoulders shuddered slightly. Swiftly turning her keen gaze in his direction, she traced with her eyes the outline of his tense jaw. Without doubt, she immediately saw through the dark, heavy quality given off by his moderate turn of phrase. Kōji recognized in Yūko's powers of intuition a sign of her love for him, and he felt overjoyed. If that were not the case, then why had they been brought together in an instant by this delicate spider's thread that was barely visible in the failing light?

Yūko seemed to waver ever so slightly in the face of Kōji's words, which revealed a quality like a darkly glittering mineral.

However, there must have been a tacit understanding between them for quite some time even before Kōji spoke.

They continued to walk at Ippei's pace, while Yūko closed her eyes with a sweep of her long eyelashes. When she opened them again, the distant embers of the sunset burned like fire in her eyes. Kōji realized then that she had changed, and she was no longer the desultory and insincere woman she had been. She had been transformed into a vibrant woman brimming with immeasurable energy.

Then she spoke. "Yes, I agree with you. In which case, you'd better come along, Kōji. And so had I. There's no going back now after all of this."

When they arrived at the harbor, Ippei, of course, was exhausted, as were they all. The light was failing, and only the crests of the waves in the bay caught the dying light.

The lighthouse shone brightly, and while it was difficult to tell the extent of the fan-shaped band of light that swept across the harbor and promontory opposite, every two seconds the flash of light clearly illuminated both the vessels that lay at anchor and also the oil tanks on the shore opposite.

Leaning against an oil drum, Ippei slid down and collapsed into a sitting position. Yūko squatted next to him, while Kōji stood alone to one side. Fanned by the cool evening breeze, the three gazed without seeing at the scenery on the dark shore in the distance.

"We haven't been over to the other side yet, have we? Let's get Teijirō to row us over one of these days in the sculling boat. We should take lots of pictures. The middle of the day would be best, though it may be hot," said Yūko.

Epilogue

I have always been interested in the traditional performing arts of celebration—so much so, in fact, that, having been encouraged in this direction at university by Professor Matsuyama, I decided on the "Study of Celebration and Reciters" as the title of my thesis.

After graduating, I took a job teaching in a high school, and during my vacation I visited my alma mater and sought the advice of Professor Matsuyama in connection with my research aims. For me, going on a research field trip was the greatest pleasure. It is fair to say that for a scholar of ethnology, the real delight is not in carrying out one's studies in the research office, but rather, in having opportunities to spend time in the field.

I spent one summer in the 1960s traveling the length and breadth of the Izu Peninsula on just this sort of fact-finding trip.

By its very nature, a peninsula is a repository for all manner of folklore material, into which flow a great many customs. These customs take root and are handed down orally with the result that unexpected folklore discoveries are made in some surprising places. Everywhere one goes in Izu, belief in the traveler's guardian deity Dōsojin is widespread. Deities such as these, which are known as "Sai no Kami," are protectors from harm and usually manifest themselves in the form of three-dimensional stone statues—designed to ward off incursions into the area by intruders from other regions. There is even a curious custom whereby, when the catch has been poor, the local children hurl the stone statue into the sea as a means of teasing and taking out their revenge on the gods.

Interestingly, there are many "Sanbasō" pieces from celebratory Noh dramas remaining in the Izu Peninsula, and this makes it a suitable location for surveying the extent to which songs of blessing and celebration are alive among the coastal-dwelling village people.

Being interested in the custom practiced in Kuri Village, West Izu, whereby, during a boat-launching ceremony, the young wife and daughter of the boat owner are thrown from the newly constructed vessel into the water (according to one theory—the vestiges of the tradition of human sacrifice), and concerned also with the boat-launching songs that are recited on such occasions, I went first to Kuri Village, following an introduction by a certain person. Timing my visit to coincide with the boat-launching ceremony, I stayed several days there and witnessed this unusual custom with my own eyes and also listened to the songs that were recited to me by the village elders. But the boat launching song had become somewhat popularized, and since it no longer resembled the original from ancient times, I was not at all satisfied with its performance.

From Kuri I took the bus and traveled due north along the coast road and arrived in the next small fishing village, called Iro. Unable to rely on the good offices of an introducer, I explained the objective of my field trip to the proprietor of the hotel I was staying at and asked whether there was an elder who passed on the oral tradition of reciting old folk songs. The proprietor said that, while he himself did not know, he was on friendly terms with the chief priest of the local Taisenji temple—Kakujin—and that, since the priest himself was interested in matters such as this, it would be more expedient to meet with him.

As I was tired, I spent that evening in the hotel putting in order the materials I had collated.

The following day was a hot midsummer's day, and after breakfast, I slipped on a pair of the hotel's *geta* and tottered along the prefectural highway. Turning right, I went past the post office before turning left again and passing through the old main gate of the Rinzai sect Taisenji temple.

A lot of children were playing in the temple precincts, and while the temple itself looked as though it had been remodeled a number of times, it still retained the majesty of the old architecture, built in the Oei era. Asking to be shown the way, I met the priest Kakujin for the first time.

During my stay in Iro Village, I was deeply impressed by the priest's character, and even during that short period, there developed between us a particularly intimate friendship; as for the priest, he no doubt welcomed me as an appreciative acquaintance at the very time he was lamenting the fact that with each passing day the young people of the village were increasingly turning their backs on the customs and traditions of the past.

Soon after our first meeting, the priest complained to me about how the boatman's song, which had been preserved by the village shrine, was on the verge of dying out, and sending for the last reciter, he arranged for him to recite the song especially for my benefit. I was truly delighted at this.

The old fisherman who soon turned up, however, was a simple soul indeed; he made the introductory remark that lately he had been suffering from ill health, the tone of his voice was disappointing, and that this would, in any case, likely be his last recital.

While the boat event itself had since died out, up until several decades ago a festival was held annually on November 3. The shrine boat *Shinkosen Myojin-maru* was splendidly decorated; the young villagers would take up its twelve pairs of oars and row around the interior of the bay all day long.

In the middle of the boat was a room of approximately fifty square feet. Inside it, five singers would recite sacred songs, and when the recital came to an end, dancers dressed in red kimonos performed a monkey dance. This was likely as not a variation of the *Noh Sanbasō* performance. It seems to be similar to the *Sanba Sarugaku* performance that still exists throughout northern Japan.

Twelve songs—beginning with the "Sacred Boat Song"— have been handed down, and it took two days to finish reciting them aboard ship. However, the only one I was able to listen to was the "Sacred Boat Song," also known as the "Song of the Gods."

Before the reciter began his recital, I had an opportunity to copy some of the verses, which were written on an old sheet of calligraphy paper.

The lyrics begin with "How joyous and happy a celebration. Yes, this is a celebration . . ." and is a typical celebratory song, devoid of any particularly notable characteristics, found throughout the various regions.

What a celebration.
In the snows of early spring,
Scarlet buds like braided joints of armor
Turn into cherry blossoms in the city.

Cascading deutzia in summer
Becomes the waterfall to the Arashi River.

When autumn comes,
The Nishiki River battles through
The eternally triumphant colors of the maple leaves.
In winter, the sky clears after the snow . . .

The song continues in a similar vein with descriptions of the four seasons, which immediately reminded me of the piece in the Collection of Sacred Celebration Songs called "On the Beach." It includes the following words: "How pleasant are the valleys!"

The valley of plums in bloom in spring.
The neighboring villages are fragrant, too.

The cool dale of fans in summer
Enjoy dayflowers in the sedge valley in autumn.
The dale of tortoise under the snow in winter;
To find it after a long absence!

The celebratory song "On the Beach" can also be found in the repertoire of the Kowaka School of Dance. Of course this piece is derived from one in the Collection of Sacred Celebration Songs; however, the version in the Collection of Sacred Celebration Songs clearly praises the city of Kamakura.

"Now that I have taken my revenge on my enemy and have made a name for myself, I can lay down my swords, bows, and arrows."

These words from the "Sacred Boat Song" reminded me of the piece called "The Celebration of a Long Life and Vengeance" in Kumiodori dance. However, the warmongering samurai vengeance theme quickly dissolves into a peaceful chant that celebrates longevity.

The reciter once again excused his poor voice and started reciting the first line of the "Sacred Boat Song" in a relaxed manner. His voice was unexpectedly beautiful. Although it was somehow melancholy, still it retained the sparkling brightness of a calm sea.

I was thrilled with the materials I had collected relating to the "Sacred Boat Song," and so I felt like staying on awhile in this village and unearthing more buried folklore materials at my leisure. Chatting with the priest during my frequent visits to Taisenji, I searched for clues in everything he said, clues that might lead to still further discoveries.

It was my fifth night since I came to the village. Having been treated to some sake at the temple and while talking with the priest about this and that, my attention was drawn in an unexpected direction by an anecdote he shared. Straying from my scholarly interests, I was seized with a burning curiosity about an incident that happened in this village two years ago. It involved a young man who, together with a married woman, strangled the woman's husband. The husband had been suffering from aphasia—the illness caused in the first place two years earlier as a result of an injury inflicted by the young man. Pressing the priest, I persuaded him to tell me everything he knew about it. Strangely, the priest shared his sympathy equally with each of these three characters, and in particular, my interest was considerably piqued by the woman called Yūko.

Even with the benefit of the priest's detailed explanation, both Yūko's appearance and her character remained enveloped in a veil of obscurity and the only image I could conjure of her was her thin lips, adorned—as they always were—with heavy lipstick.

This vague image, which was so difficult to grasp, was for me just like an old and beautiful, and yet mysterious, piece of folklore that had been buried, and what a valuable scholarly discovery it would be, if only I could capture it now, when it was on the point of being lost—having been passed down in the utmost secrecy.

Then at last, the priest suggested he show me a photograph that was in his possession. As he stood up to open the box where it was kept, I felt overwhelmed with feelings of both hope and unease. Researchers like me often experience disappointment on field trips when, leaving aside the collation of data relating to the oral transmission of language and thought, we are dismayed to find that a particular ancient manuscript that has been described to us in glowing terms actually turns out to be nothing remarkable.

I was afraid that Yūko's actual photograph would fall short of my expectations. Fortunately, my fears proved groundless.

Besides its being slightly overexposed, the three figures in the picture wore white clothing, accentuating the brightness of the photograph all the more. Despite this, the picture was distinct and above all else the friendly intimacy created a strange impression. Yūko was in the middle of the frame, wearing a white dress and smiling, holding a folded parasol in her hand.

If anything, her generously proportioned, gay face gave off a hint of unrefined but graceful sorrow, and while thin, her lips were also beautiful. Delighted that my illusion had not been shattered, at the same time I knew full well that the priest's storytelling contained no exaggeration.

The photograph had been nonchalantly given to the priest the day before the incident, when Kōji made his customary delivery of flowers to the temple. With the benefit of hindsight, no doubt everyone would agree that this was a suggestive gift indeed. More will be said about this later. The most pronounced impression was left by the priest's description of Kōji and Yūko the morning after the murder. Being an early riser, the priest was in the habit of going down into the back garden of the temple before daybreak and puttering around.

The sky was beginning to lighten. Just then he became aware of footsteps coming down the slope that led back up to the Kusakado greenhouse and looked up from what he was doing. Usually, no one came down from the house this early in the morning. When he looked again, he realized it was Yūko and Kōji, holding hands as they came toward him. Just at that moment, a flash of light from the eastern mountains illuminated the slope, signaling the arrival of dawn, and the couple appeared brilliantly lit in the first light of day.

Their faces brimming with happiness, and with a youthful spring in their step, they appeared more beautiful than ever before. Descending the dew-wet path, surrounded by the lingering cries of the morning insects, Yūko and Kōji truly looked like bride and groom . . .

The priest could be forgiven for thinking that they were the bearers of extraordinarily glad tidings. In fact, however, they had come to ask him to accompany them to the police station, where they intended to turn themselves in. They confessed to strangling Ippei to death late the previous night using a thin length of cord. Moreover, Kōji claimed that he had carried out the murder at Ippei's request. The priest testified that around noon on the previous day, Kōji had given him the photograph when he came to deliver the flowers. It seems that this was Kōji's attempt to allude to the fact that it wasn't an impulsive crime, but rather one committed at the victim's behest.

However, since there was no circumstantial evidence, let alone any direct evidence, supporting his explanation, Kōji's plea was rejected. Instead, the strange gift of the photograph was seen as proof of the premeditated nature of the crime. Kōji and Yūko were regarded as complicit. Kōji had a previous conviction for bodily harm against the victim, and accordingly there was no chance to plead extenuating circumstances. He was given the death penalty, and Yūko was sentenced to life imprisonment.

Subsequently, Kōji and Yūko both sent letters to the priest from prison, imploring him to somehow arrange for their graves to be erected side by side. While this appeared a strange request, the priest discerned that behind it lay the specter of some mournful hope. Perhaps herein lay the real motive for delivering the photograph the day before the crime was committed.

However, setting aside the question of Ippei's grave, the issue of placing the other two graves side by side encountered intense resistance from certain influential villagers, and so the priest was forced to wait and bide his time.

Last autumn, Kōji was finally executed.

In the early spring of this year, as the three had wished, the priest arranged for Yūko's commemorative headstone to be built to the left of Ippei's grave—which already stood there—and to the left of that, for Kōji's tombstone to be erected.

Guided by the priest, I paid a visit to the three mysterious graves, and having obtained permission, I took a photograph. As if he had perceived my thoughts, as I did so the priest casually approached me with the following request. He explained that the reason he had not yet sent a photograph of the graves to Yūko was that, if possible, he had wanted to visit her and deliver it in person, but since it had been rather difficult to find an opportunity to do so, he asked if I might go in his place. I readily agreed.

As a result of this, my summer field trip came to an end having yielded an unexpectedly poor harvest. My thoughts continually ran ahead to the meeting with Yūko, and since learning of this story from the priest, I lost interest in devoting myself to my research.

Following my return to Tokyo, with just a few days left before the end of the summer vacation, I decided that at last today would be the day I would pay a visit to Tochigi prison.

At Asakusa I boarded a train on the Tobu line bound for Nikko Kinugawa, alighting onto the platform of Tochigi station at 1:59 p.m.

The lingering summer heat was relentless. Several swallows—which showed no sign of leaving soon—busily flew in and out of the old eaves above the station entrance. The sun was dazzling, and the sweeping shadows of the swallows skimmed past my eyes like a handful of small stones that had been hurled in the air before plummeting onto the deserted white square in front of the station.

The eaves of the houses were low. To the right could be seen the foliage of a row of shabby roadside trees along the wide sidewalk that led to the shopping district. Just like in any provincial city, here, too, were dozens of incongruously large buses lined up, displaying their grandeur. I boarded the bus for Oyama, as I had been instructed to by the priest. With just a few passengers on board, the bus made its way through the shopping district, where, it being afternoon on a Monday, the stores were mostly closed. There was a noodle bar that had a cascade of red roses trailing over a black fence. There was hardly anyone walking along the street. The monotonous sunlight shone relentlessly.

The bus, having gone briefly to the outskirts of the town— which had become disagreeably hot—and picked up some passengers, now returned the way it had come, turning left at the telephone and telegram exchange—situated midway along the shopping street—and then entered an unpaved road. The bus shook terribly.

"The next stop is the prison. Are there any passengers stopping at the prison?" announced a young female conductor, glancing at my face. I was surprised to feel a sense of embarrassment—as if I were doing something a little questionable—feelings I imagined were experienced by any visitor going to see a female relative in this women's prison. These past few weeks, Yūko, whom I had not yet seen, occupied my thoughts almost night and day.

The bus passed by the front of several buildings—the court-house, with its large protruding gables like a Buddhist temple, a law office, and the prison caterer—before stopping at the foot of a small stone bridge. Turning right at the approach to the bridge, a private road, ten yards in width, led straight to the front gate of the prison. Cherry trees lined the road on either side, although they were still saplings.

The official residences of officers such as the prison governor and chief warden were located in this area, and beyond, the prison was surrounded by a high wall constructed of Oyaishi stone. There was no sign of life at all here either.

When I got down from the bus, I was amazed to hear dozens of twittering birds. I couldn't see them, but they sounded like sparrows. Starting with the garden in front of the courthouse, there were many ancient trees in this vicinity, and not only that, but the songbirds appeared to be nesting in the invisible nooks and crannies of the old houses.

As I drew near the prison ahead, I saw that the leaves of the green door set between large stone gateposts were shut, and the gables of the old entrance—reminiscent of Meiji period architecture—stood imposingly before me. Dark treetops of Japanese cypress were conspicuous from the gates. Entering through a side door on the right, I stated the purpose of my visit to the gatekeeper. I had to submit my application for a visit at the general affairs section window at the rear of the main entrance hall.

Upon going inside the gloomy interior, having walked past the entrance pillars, with their large copper decorative nail head covers, I saw a showcase containing items manufactured by the inmates, such as sash fasteners, handbags, gloves, ties, socks, sweaters, and blouses.

I took a visiting request form from the general affairs section window, and while writing in the columns such details as the inmate's name, the nature of the visit, and the visitor's relationship with the inmate, I suddenly noticed a magnificent Confederate rose in a vase for a single flower on one corner of a shelf.

I was surprised to find a flower as graceful as this in a prison, and in looking at it, I felt acutely aware of the fact that only female inmates were interned here and that it was a dwelling place for those with worldly desires, and also that somewhere at the back of this gloomy building was Yūko.

I handed in my written application at the window, having attached to it a letter from the priest (who was now Yūko's guardian) written in courteous terms and explaining that I was his representative—making the visit for the purposes of enlightening the prisoner by delivering a photograph of the graves. I was told to go to the waiting room.

Once more I went out into the dazzling outdoors and entered a small waiting room just inside the gates. There was no one there either. Some infused barley tea had been prepared, and so, wiping the perspiration from my brow, I drank down a cup with relish.

I waited, wondering if I was ever going to be summoned. Everywhere was still in the late-summer sunlight; it was difficult to imagine there were crowds of women in the building beyond.

I beguiled my time by gazing at a notice on the wall, which read:

If you have been waiting more than 30 minutes please inquire with the desk clerk.

Persons other than family members and guardians, as well as persons below the age of 14, are not permitted to visit.

Please refrain from speaking in a foreign language or discussing matters not listed on the interview application form.

I was afraid that perhaps my interview might not be allowed. After all, I was a stranger to the prisoner—nothing more than

the representative of another, and handing over items during
the visit was no doubt prohibited. Then again, the priest had
already met once or twice with the prison governor and subsequently corresponded frequently by letter also; there ought
to have been, therefore, a considerable degree of trust between
the two.

I waited in the suffocating heat. Cicadas sang. A number of
illusory images merged, and my head swam.

At last, my name was called out. A female warden, dressed
in semiformal uniform—a white short-sleeved summer top
and trousers—called over to me from the green door of a booth
several yards to the front.

As I approached, she spoke quickly and in a low voice. "The
various conditions attached to your visit are quite exacting, but
permission has been expressly granted. First of all, would you
please show me the photograph of the graves?"

I showed the warden the photograph that I had taken myself.
She simply said, "Please—you should give it to her yourself," before inviting me through to the visiting room. The
interior of the room was a little over sixty square feet. There
was a table in the middle, positioned flush against the wall,
and the gap between the table legs was securely boarded up
to prevent anyone surreptitiously passing articles underneath.
The table was covered with a white vinyl cover, and next to
the wall was an arrangement of four-o'clocks with small white
flowers. A calendar and a crude framed picture of roses, among
other things, hung on the wall. The windows, which had been
left open, were adjacent to the wall of the old building and so
didn't allow the draft to come through from outside.

There were two chairs on either side of the table, and I sat
down on the one nearest the edge of the table and farthest from
the wall. The warden stood by the window. There was a door at

the back of the room. Beyond the plain glass, it was dark and of no help whatsoever—all I could see was my own reflection.

Before long, I heard the creak of a door being opened, and a dull light shone through the glass. It seemed there was a farther door after this one that led through to the room beyond. A pale face appeared through the glass, and the door opened widely and roughly toward me.

Accompanied by another female warden, Yūko appeared, wearing casual summer clothes—a blue, short-sleeved dress, gathered at the hem and with the collar adjusted like that of a kimono.

Then, looking at me, she greeted me politely in a manner appropriate for a first meeting and sat down opposite me with the warden to her side. The other warden remained standing beside the window.

I took a furtive look at Yūko's face as she hung her head. It was quite unremarkable. She had round, generously proportioned features: fleshy, as if swollen, and while her skin was well cared for and pale and tender, her thin lips—devoid of lipstick—described a hard line across the lower half of her face, giving her a coarse appearance. Her eyebrows were fine, although spread out and indistinct to the point that they emphasized her deeply sunken eyes. Her hair done up in a Western style, without so much as a strand out of place, made her fleshy face look all the more severe. Her body, too, had run to loose fat, and her bare arms had an extremely heavy look about them.

My first impression was that this woman was without question no longer young. I took out the photograph and, having passed on a message from the priest, explained the circumstances by which I had come to deliver it on his behalf.

Even while listening to my story, Yūko remained with her

eyes cast down and thanked me repeatedly. Her voice was not how I imagined it would be either.

At length, she reached out her hand and took the photograph from the tabletop. Holding it by the edges, her body bent forward, she stared intently at it. She spent such a long time looking at it that I was afraid the warden would intervene. When she had finished looking at it she placed it back on the table and gazed at it wistfully as if reluctant to part with it.

"Thank you very much," she said. "Now I can serve my time in peace. Please convey my best wishes to the priest." Yūko's words broke off, and taking a handkerchief from her pocket, she busily dabbed at her eyes. "I can put my mind at rest, now that you have done this for me. We truly were close friends, you know. The closest there can be. You can understand that, I'm sure. Only the priest knew about it. You understand, don't you?"

Before long, the warden announced that visiting time was up. In tears, Yūko nodded repeatedly, placed the card-size photograph in her pocket, and picked up her handkerchief without returning it to her pocket to prevent the photograph getting wet. From somewhere nearby, the high-pitched chirr of a cicada sounded irritatingly in my ear.

Yūko stood up, bowed deeply to me, and went through the door the warden had opened. Through the glass I could still see her blue casual clothes and the white nape of her neck. For an instant, it drifted distinctly by on the other side of the vibrating glass. But the door at the back had been opened, and when it closed again, Yūko's form had gone from my sight.

Translator's Note:
The Origins of The Frolic of the Beasts

Yukio Mishima was an avowed fan of traditional Japanese Noh theater, and in fact, he wrote several Noh plays himself. *The Frolic of the Beasts* is considered a parody of the classical Noh play *Motomezuka*, written in the fourteenth century by the playwright Kiyotsugu Kan'ami.

Motomezuka tells the story of a priest and his companions who journey from the western provinces to Kyoto but stop en route in the village of Ikuta in Settsu Province. There they encounter several village girls who relate to them the story of the maiden Unai.

In the girls' telling, Unai is courted by two young men from the village, Sasada and Chinu. Loath to declare her love for one and disappoint the other, she ignores their overtures. Her parents intervene and attempt to resolve the impasse by having the suitors compete for her hand, but each contest ends in a draw. Finding herself in an impossible quandary, Unai plunges into the Ikuta River and kills herself. Brokenhearted, Sasada and Chinu follow suit, stabbing each other to death and descending to hell.

The priest chants prayers for the repose of Unai's soul but to no avail; she is powerless to break her attachment to the Burning House (a Buddhist metaphor for the secular world) and the Eight Great Hells, through which she must endure unending torment by her demons.

The love triangle between Unai, Sasada, and Chinu is mirrored in the novel in the relationship between Yūko, Ippei, and Kōji, as well as in Kiyoshi's and Matsukichi's courtship of Kimi.

Noh productions are characterized by their use of highly stylized masks that represent specific characters, and references to these masks can be found throughout *The Frolic of the Beasts*. Kōji remarks that his own face "is like a well-crafted, carved wooden mask," and the "interminable smile" worn by Ippei recalls the fixed expression of a Noh mask. Similarly, Yūko's defining feature, her thick, dark lipstick, is likely a direct reference to the quintessential "young woman" character found in Noh theater.

—ANDREW CLARE,
May 2018

FIVE MODERN NŌ PLAYS

Japanese Nō drama is one of the world's great art forms. Yukio Mishima, one of Japan's outstanding postwar writers, infused new life into the form by using it for plays that preserve the style and inner spirit of Nō but are at the same time so modern, so direct, and intelligible that they could, as he suggested, be played on a bench in Central Park. Here are five of his Nō plays, stunning in their contemporary nature and relevance—and finally made available again for readers to enjoy.

Drama

FORBIDDEN COLORS

From one of Japan's greatest modern writers comes an exquisitely disturbing novel of sexual combat and concealed passion, a work that distills beauty, longing, and loathing into an intoxicating poisoned cocktail. An aging, embittered novelist sets out to avenge himself on the women who have betrayed him. He finds the perfect instrument in Yuichi, a young man whose beauty makes him irresistible to women but who is just discovering his attraction to other men. As Yuichi's mentor presses him into a loveless marriage and a series of equally loveless philanderings, his protégé enters the gay underworld of postwar Japan. In that hidden society of parks and tearooms, prostitutes and aristocratic blackmailers, Yuichi is as defenseless as any of the women he preys on. Mordantly observed, intellectually provocative, and filled with icy eroticism, *Forbidden Colors* is a masterpiece.

Fiction

Thirteen-year-old Noboru is a member of a gang of highly philosophical teenage boys who reject the tenets of the adult world—to them, adult life is illusory, hypocritical, and sentimental. When Noboru's widowed mother is romanced by Ryuji, a sailor, Noboru is thrilled. He idolizes this rugged man of the sea as a hero. But his admiration soon turns to hatred as Ryuji forsakes life on board the ship for marriage, rejecting everything Noboru holds sacred. Upset and appalled, he and his friends respond to this apparent betrayal with a terrible ferocity.

Fiction

HB 02.21.2023 1307

VINTAGE INTERNATIONAL
Available wherever books are sold.
www.vintagebooks.com